A terrible change had come over the bay

And the sea! Where a calm blue pool had been earlier, there was now a boiling mass of white-and-green waves.

"It's a summer gale," he grated. "I've been a fool! I didn't think to listen for a gale warning—we were going such a short distance!" A sudden crack above the roar of the coming storm drew their attention to the boat. "I've got to try to cut it loose!" he yelled.

"No—Carlo!" She watched in terror as he struggled with the mooring rope, waist deep in the swirling water.

The blackness of the sky was suddenly split with a livid flash of lightning, followed almost at once by a crash of thunder.

Kate screamed, and at the same time Carlo lost his footing in the wild evil water.

WELCOME
TO THE WONDERFUL WORLD
OF *Harlequin Presents*

Interesting, informative and entertaining,
each Harlequin Presents portrays an appealing
and original love story. With a varied array
of settings, we may lure you on an African safari,
to a quaint Welsh village, or an exotic Riviera
location—anywhere and everywhere that adventurous
men and women fall in love.

As publishers of Harlequin Presents, we're
extremely proud of our books. Since 1949,
Harlequin Enterprises has built its publishing
reputation on the solid base of quality and
originality. Our stories are the most popular
paperback romances sold in North America; every
month, eight new titles are released and sold at
nearly every book-selling store in Canada and the
United States.

A free catalogue listing all Harlequin Presents
can be yours by writing to the

HARLEQUIN READER SERVICE,
(In the U.S.) 2504 West Southern Avenue, Tempe, AZ 85282
(In Canada) Stratford, Ontario, N5A 6W2

We sincerely hope you enjoy reading
this Harlequin Presents.

Yours truly,

THE PUBLISHERS
Harlequin Presents

MADELEINE KER

aquamarine

Harlequin Books

TORONTO • NEW YORK • LONDON
AMSTERDAM • PARIS • SYDNEY • HAMBURG
STOCKHOLM • ATHENS • TOKYO • MILAN

Harlequin Presents first edition November 1983
ISBN 0-373-10642-4

Original hardcover edition published in 1983
by Mills & Boon Limited

Printed in U.S.A.

CHAPTER ONE

'IN the absence of Signor Castelli,' said the lawyer, consulting his absurdly old-fashioned fob-watch, 'I think we had better begin.'

'Quite so,' said Vera de Cruz. 'It's getting late, and Signor Castelli can always pick up the details later. Don't you agree, my dear?' She turned her glistening black eyes on the English girl who was sitting in the third chair in front of the lawyer's desk.

'If you like,' said Kate. 'I don't suppose Signor Castelli will mind.'

'Sensible girl,' purred Vera de Cruz, turning back to the lawyer. 'Go ahead, Mr Potter—read the will.'

Sebastian Potter, the senior partner of Potter, Bush & Linford, picked up the red-sealed envelope, and looked at the two women in his office, absently noting the fresh beauty of the one, and contrasting it with the hothouse sultriness of the other. His normally impassive face wore an expression of faint disapproval. It was an expression which had been perfected over years of court-room practise. It had informed many a jury, more plainly than any words, that the prosecution's testimony was utterly absurd, worthless, a fabricated concoction of insane lies. It was a devastating expression. And it had been worth more to Sebastian Potter—in terms of convinced juries and acquitted clients—than the most expensive legal training. But at this moment, the expression on the lawyer's face was unfeigned.

'Before I proceed to explain my client's will,' he began,

'I should inform both of you ladies that I am fully acquainted with its contents. I helped Mr Roger Courtney draw it up. And I must tell you that I disapproved most strongly of the course Mr Courtney wished to take. It struck me as most eccentric.'

'Eccentric?' said Vera de Cruz, gold cigarette-lighter poised in scarlet-nailed fingers. A hard edge crept into her plummy voice. 'Eccentric in what way, Mr Potter?'

The lawyer held up a thin hand.

'You will see in a moment, Miss de Cruz. Please be patient. Now, Miss Melville.' He turned to the other person in the room. 'Mr Courtney was your uncle, was he not?'

'Yes,' nodded Kate, remembering a childhood vision of a delightfully mischievous grown-up who understood so well what made children laugh.

'Did you see him over the last years of his life?'

'No.' She frowned thoughtfully. 'The last time I saw him was when I was eight or nine. After the quarrel with my father, Uncle Roger never came back to our house. And as he grew more eccentric in his middle age, he simply refused to see anyone. I used to write to him regularly, and he would answer now and then. But I never saw him.'

'Roger was a nutcase,' said Vera smoothly, exhaling a plume of smoke. 'Pure and simple. Hiding himself away on that island like that—it was ridiculous!'

'I am inclined to agree with you, Miss de Cruz,' said Sebastian Potter. 'Your cousin had some very peculiar notions. I found it all most irregular. And it was all the more unsatisfactory,' added the lawyer, looking down at the will, 'when one considered the very large size of the estate he possessed.'

'You don't say,' drawled Vera, glancing over at Kate with glittering eyes. 'Did you know the old man was wealthy?'

'Well,' said Kate, brushing the blonde hair away from her temples, 'I knew that he owned that island off Sicily; but I never really thought about Uncle Roger in terms of money.'

'You astonish me.' Vera's immaculately made-up face registered scepticism so perfectly that Sebastian Potter felt quite a pang of professional jealousy. She blew out another feather of smoke, and raised one eyebrow at the lawyer. 'Well, Mr Potter, we all agree that Roger was off his rocker. And Mr Castelli *still* hasn't arrived. So why don't you spill the beans?'

'Very well, Miss de Cruz.' Mr Potter broke the brittle seal and pulled the will out of its envelope. 'The wording is rather complicated, Miss de Cruz and Miss Melville. Would you like me to explain what it says in layman's terms before I read it out?'

'Yes, please,' said Kate. She folded her hands, wondering what Roger Courtney's last joke was going to entail. Because she was quite convinced that Roger's will would embody the mocking, teasing attitude with which he had always treated a family who misunderstood him. Although she had not seen him for so many years, Kate knew that of the whole family, she was the only one who felt any inkling of understanding for Roger Courtney. In the few letters he had sent her, she had seen the lonely plight of a truly loving and mischievous man who had simply been too unconventional for a stuffy English family. Uncle Roger had been a forbidden topic in her parents' household and it had taken her years to learn of the passionate affair with a married woman which had first ostracised him from his community. And the bouts of excitability which had necessitated psychiatric treatment. And the sparkling practical jokes which had so infuriated his staid relations. And the drinking. And the car-crashes. And all the other hundreds of things which made Roger Courtney impossible—simply impossible—as a relation in middle-class Surrey. Perhaps with the onset of mellow middle age, her mother and her erratic uncle might have been reconciled, and Roger might have been drawn back into the bosom of his family; but that was not to be. Kate's parents had died instantly when the lorry met their car head-on in a peaceful country lane, a leafy and bird-haunted spot that was scarcely suitable for dying in on a summer afternoon. And Roger Courtney had remained in exile on his little island off Sicily. But Kate had never forgotten the pathetic letter he had sent her when the news of her parents' death had reached him. And now that Roger himself was at peace, Kate had not the slightest doubt that any will he had left would be as wickedly mischievous as the man himself had been in life.

'There are three beneficiaries,' said Mr Potter in his quiet, precise way. 'Miss Katherine Melville, his niece; Miss Vera de Cruz, his cousin; and Signor Carlo Castelli. Now—'

'Burning with curiosity though I am,' drawled Vera, brushing invisible specks off her expensive wool skirt, 'before we hear Roger's will, might we know exactly who Signor Carlo Castelli *is?*'

Mr Potter sighed inwardly. 'That will become clear when I read out Mr Courtney's will, Miss de Cruz. In the meantime, I can tell you that Signor Castelli is—was, I should say, a close friend of your cousin's.'

Vera's eyebrow lifted fractionally again, and again Mr

Potter was struck with admiration. An eyebrow like that, he reflected, could win cases in the criminal courts. Vera gave Kate the benefit of her eyebrow.

'Have *you* heard of this mysterious gentleman, Katherine?'

'Well, yes—in a way,' acknowledged Kate. 'Uncle Roger did mention him two or three times as being a good friend. But I don't know who he is.'

'You don't?' The eyebrow was still sceptical as Vera turned back to Sebastian Potter. 'Please go on, Mr Potter.'

Somewhat dreading the reaction he was going to get, Mr Potter tapped the will gently on to his desk.

'I say that there are three beneficiaries, but to be absolutely precise, my dear ladies, there are only two. You see, Mr Courtney left a somewhat unusual provision in his will. And I am not entirely displeased that Mr Castelli should be absent for the opening of the will.' Mr Potter cleared his throat gently. 'His presence might have proved something of an embarrassment.'

'Mr Potter,' murmured Vera, her eyes fixed on the lawyer's face intently, 'you alarm me inexpressibly.'

'The bulk of Roger Courtney's estate, Miss Melville and Miss de Cruz, consists of the island of Leparú, which is off the coast of Sicily, and a number of buildings which Mr Courtney had erected there. What Mr Courtney's will states is this: that the island, and everything on it, will immediately devolve to any two of the three beneficiaries who are married to one another within one year of this date.'

There was a complete silence for several seconds after this statement. Suddenly Kate Melville grinned. And at the same moment, Vera de Cruz's eyebrows both began a steady upward climb which gave her an extraordinarily doll-like look.

'Ah well,' sighed Kate, 'I couldn't quite see myself as the mistress of an Aeolian island, anyhow.'

'You're not having a little joke, are you, Mr Potter?' asked Vera in a freezing voice.

Sebastian Potter shook his head. 'I'm afraid not, Miss de Cruz. That is exactly what Mr Courtney's will states.' He cleared his throat again. 'It means, in effect, that the island of Leparú will belong to whichever of you two ladies marries Signor Castelli. Within the stated period, of course.' He folded his hands.

Vera's face was pale with anger.

'Does Castelli know this?' she snapped.

'Oh no, Miss de Cruz. Signor Castelli has yet to hear the terms of the will.'

Vera whipped round to face Kate. 'And what do you know about this, Katherine?'

'Nothing, Vera.' Kate looked calmly into Vera's dark eyes. 'Uncle Roger was addicted to practical jokes—you know that. Well, this is his last little prank.'

'Prank?' snapped Vera. 'Some prank!'

'Miss de Cruz is correct, Miss Melville.' Mr Potter watched them both speculatively. 'You uncle's will is not entirely a joke. As it stands, it is of course quite legal. And Mr Courtney left no conditions about the length the marriage had to last.'

Vera's expression changed abruptly. 'What are you saying, Mr Potter?'

'I am simply pointing out that Leparú is an extremely valuable property, Miss de Cruz. I don't have any estimates, but it's easily worth several hundred thousand pounds. Perhaps over a quarter of a million.'

Vera's eyes glittered. 'God! And it seems that this Castelli can't lose?'

'Signor Castelli cannot inherit without the—er—co-operation of one of you,' Mr Potter pointed out. 'But marriage—and divorce—is not a difficult matter in certain countries.' He looked at them both. 'It will certainly be worth discussing the matter with Signor Castelli, when he makes himself available.' There was another pause.

'Mr Potter,' asked Kate, 'what if there's no marriage?'

'In that case, Leparú will be turned into a home for retired donkeys.' There was the ghost of a chuckle, and to her surprise, Kate realized that it had come from Mr Potter. Vera looked across at Kate with bright eyes.

'Interesting situation, eh, Katherine?'

'Very,' said Kate calmly. 'Uncle Roger was an expert at setting up interesting situations.'

'Let me explain the rest of the will, ladies. It's not complicated, but I want you to understand your position perfectly.' Mr Potter took three envelopes out of a file on his desk. 'In the first place, there is a small package for each of you, from Mr Courtney. I may tell you that each one contains a letter, and a banker's draft for quite a generous sum of money. I'm going to give you yours now.' Kate took the envelope, and held it in her lap. In her uncle's familiar writing, the name *Caterina Melville* was scrawled across the front. It had been the name by which he addressed her in his odd, delightful letters.

'In the second place,' continued the lawyer, 'provision has been made for all of you to visit Leparú at any time within the next six months. You may stay there as long as you like. The island, the houses on it, and all the servants, will be completely at your disposal. There are many more minor details, but we'll come to them later—they're not important. Do you both understand what I've said?'

'Perfectly,' said Vera. Her dark eyes were inward-looking, and a smile was curving her glossy lips. Mr Potter turned to Kate.

'Yes,' she nodded, 'I understand, Mr Potter.'

'Good. And now I'd better read the will.'

Sebastian Potter had been very thorough.

'"My good and true friend, Carlo Castelli",' quoted Vera, looking at Kate. 'Well, my dear Katherine, it seems that Signor Castelli holds the key to our futures.'

'*Our* futures?' queried Kate, returning Vera's gaze. 'Whoever Signor Castelli may be, Vera, he has no possible connection with my future.'

'Oh, nonsense, girl!' Vera shot a quick look at Mr Potter, then stood up. 'Let's go and have a drink somewhere—just you and I. Mr Potter, we're grateful to you for all you've done.'

'Not at all, Miss de Cruz.' Mr Potter rose to usher them out of his office. 'As soon as Signor Castelli contacts me, I will let you both know. And if there's anything more you want to know, please don't hesitate to ask me.'

As they walked out into a fine London drizzle, Vera took Kate's arm firmly in one hand, and with the other signalled a passing cab. 'The Sheraton, driver,' she commanded, and pulled Kate into the back seat with her.

'Katherine, don't try to deceive me. You know more about this absurd will than you're letting on, don't you?'

'I promise you I don't,' smiled Kate. 'It's just the sort of thing Uncle Roger would do—I told you.'

'You and dear old Uncle Roger haven't cooked up some nasty scheme, have you? to trick poor Vera?'

'Vera,' said Kate patiently, looking into the older

woman's suspicious eyes, 'if Uncle Roger had decided to cut you out of his will, he would have done so, wouldn't he? There wouldn't have been any need for such an elaborate charade.'

'Then what the devil is it all about?' asked Vera plaintively. 'I must say, Katherine, you're taking this very calmly.'

'Why should I be upset? Uncle Roger's island wasn't anything to do with me. I never expected to get a penny from him.'

'Don't tell me you're not interested in a quarter of a million pounds' worth of Sicilian island,' said Vera scornfully.

Kate looked out of the window to hide her smile. As her only living relation, Vera de Cruz had a strong claim to Kate's sympathy. But it was difficult to like Vera. Beautiful in a sultry, petulant way, careful to always present a veneer of sophistication, she could on certain memorable occasions erupt into the fury of a screaming fishwife. Kate had seen her do it. And with the Spanish temper that her father had bequeathed her had come a Spanish distrust of the world. Vera was pathologically suspicious. Pretty as she was, she attracted plenty of men. But Kate was certain that the reason Vera's thirtieth birthday had come and gone with not the slightest sign of a permanent engagement was that Vera was constitutionally unable to trust any of the men who courted her.

'Naturally, I'm interested in Uncle Roger's island. But I'm not obsessed with it. I've got my own life here in London—and I'm certainly not going to enter a hollow marriage with some stranger just to make a few pounds.'

'A few pounds?' gasped Vera as they emerged from the taxi in front of the huge hotel where she had taken a room.

'You don't seem to understand the value of money, darling!'

'You mean you'd marry this Carlo Castelli—whoever he was—simply to get Leparú?'

'You're darn tooting,' said Vera briskly. 'And don't tell me you wouldn't, either, because I won't believe it.'

Over cocktails in the elegant bar, she grew solemn.

'Now listen to me, Katherine. We're going to have to come to some kind of arrangement, for all our sakes.'

'Arrangement?'

'Yes. Now, this is what I've worked out. When we meet this Castelli, we all agree to split Leparú between us, three ways. So, you and I draw lots to see which one will marry Signor Castelli. Then, before the marriage, we all sign a contract agreeing that there'll be a divorce within such and such a time, and all agreeing to sell Leparú, and split the proceeds. What do you say to that?'

'Not bad,' smiled Kate. 'But it won't work.'

'Why not?'

'Well, for one thing, it's illegal to make a contract saying you're going to divorce someone before you've even married them. And if that part of the contract was illegal, the whole thing would be null and void.'

Vera's face fell. 'Are you sure?'

'You could always check with Mr Potter. But I'm pretty sure that's right.'

'I see.' Vera sipped her crème de menthe thoughtfully.

'Uncle Roger's tricks always had subtle depths to them,' commented Kate. 'They were never quite as simple as they first seemed.'

'Yes.' Vera looked at Kate strangely. 'So—it's between you and me, Katherine.'

'What is?'

'Leparú is. Or, to be precise, Signor Carlo Castelli is.'

'I hoped you weren't going to see it like that,' sighed Kate. 'If you can persuade this Signor Castelli to marry you, Vera, good luck to you. But I'm convinced you'll be infinitely more miserable if you do so than you can possibly imagine.'

'Is that what you think?' Vera smiled at a man at a table near them, and Kate saw the man's face light up.

'Yes,' said Kate firmly. 'And please count me out of any little schemes you might be hatching.'

'Schemes?' asked Vera innocently. 'No schemes, my dear Kathcrine, I assure you. No doubt you'll want to play the field on your own.'

'There's no question of that,' said Kate patiently. 'I'm not really very interested in Uncle Roger's island.'

'Of course not,' smiled Vera, her eyebrow doing its trick again. 'You're so rich that you can do without Uncle Roger's millions, eh?'

A light flush rose to Kate's cheeks.

'I may not be very well off, Vera, but that doesn't mean I'd compromise to get rich quick.'

'Oh no,' sneered Vera. 'Saintly Kate wouldn't dirty her hands, would she—but nasty Vera would!'

'I didn't mean that, Vera, and you know it. I've told you—if you want to come to some agreement with Carlo Castelli, then do so, by all means. I don't care what you decide—I don't want Leparú. Not at that price.'

'Can I have that in writing?' asked Vera sarcastically.

Kate finished her drink, and picked up her handbag.

'Listen to me, Vera—I don't even want to see Carlo Castelli. And as for—'

'Who are you trying to kid?' Vera's face was ugly with suspicion and anger. 'You seem to attract enough boy-friends, little Miss Muffet. Men seem to go for those big blue eyes and that golden hair—and you know it. Don't try and tell me you're not going to make a play for this Castelli as soon as my back's turned!'

'And even if I was, what would you do about it? What do you expect me to say?'

'Oh, I don't know,' snapped Vera moodily. 'This whole thing is quite beyond a joke, Katherine.'

'Try and see the funny side,' advised Kate. 'Uncle Roger evidently wanted to tantalize us with this precious island of his. Can't you see that? He never intended either of us to have it. You know how shoddily the whole family treated him—well, this is his revenge on the surviving members.'

'I want that island,' said Vera petulantly. Her face was like a spoiled child's, but there was real passion in her eyes.

'You worry me sometimes, Vera. You don't know anything about this man Castelli, in any case. He might be a dreadful person. I wouldn't put it past Uncle Roger to have chosen Castelli simply because he was hideous—or an alcoholic. He could even be married already.'

A look of anguish passed over Vera's pretty face.

'Oh hell! I never thought of that. You don't think it's possible?'

'Anything's possible with Uncle Roger,' said Kate decisively. 'Though I doubt that Castelli's actually married—Uncle Roger wouldn't have been able to make the will the way he did in that case.'

'If this Castelli's a man,' swore Vera, 'I'm going to marry him. Whatever.'

'Ah well, I'm going back to my flat now. I want to read Roger's letter. But listen to one last word, Vera: I know

Uncle Roger's tricks. And take it from me, they're very seldom what they seem. There are bound to be hidden catches in this one. And considering it's his last little joke, the catches are likely to be extra-special.'

'There's nothing so special that it's going to catch Vera de Cruz.' She drank off her green cocktail, and the two women stood up. 'Katherine, let's meet again and talk this over later on. Maybe—'

'Excuse me, madam.'

'Yes?' Vera turned to the young waiter. 'What is it?'

'Are you Miss de Cruz?'

'Yes. What do you want?'

'There's a gentleman looking for you, miss—by the name of Castelli.'

Kate was aware that her heart had begun to beat a little faster. Vera glanced at her with wide, excited eyes, and then turned to the waiter. 'Where is he?'

'He's just coming now, miss. Over there.'

The two women turned to watch a tall man, all in black, making his way through the crowds towards them. A large smile was stretched across his face.

'Miss de Cruz?' he boomed, in a foreign accent. 'Mr Potter told me you might be here.' He held out a large hand. 'My name is Castelli.'

Vera had turned as white as paper. She put out a hand to steady herself on a chair. 'My God!' she breathed.

'Amen,' said Mr Castelli. Kate began to giggle helplessly. Trust Roger Courtney to have the last laugh! For Mr Castelli, who was watching the two women with an air of hurt perplexity, was dressed in the black soutane and white dog-collar of a Roman Catholic priest.

*

It was Kate who recovered first. Swallowing her laughter, she took the priest's outstretched hand.

'How do you do, Father? I'm Katherine Melville. And this is Veru de Cruz. Would you care to—er—join us for a drink?'

'Orange juice,' he boomed happily, wringing Kate's hand. 'Nothing more—not while I'm in uniform, eh?' He pulled chairs out for both of them, chuckling, and Vera sat down weakly. The colour had returned to her cheeks, and by the hunted look in her eyes, Kate guessed that she was feverishly seeking the solution to this latest obstacle. Vera leaned forward.

'Mr Castelli,' she said hesitantly, 'I mean—er—Father—you are really a father? A priest, I mean?'

'A priest? But of course I'm a priest,' said Father Castelli in some surprise. He gestured at his dog-collar. 'I've got the uniform, no?'

'Then there's no joke?'

'Joke?' asked Father Castelli. His round, honest face was beginning to be furrowed with doubt. He clearly suspected that he was dealing with two escaped lunatics.

Kate hastily intervened. 'Miss de Cruz is a little confused, Father. She'll be all right in a few minutes.'

'All right?' spluttered Vera. 'That old joker, that—'

'Here's your orange juice,' interrupted Kate in relief. 'I suppose you've just been to Potter, Bush & Linford?'

'Exactly,' said the priest. He raised his orange juice cheerfully. 'Your health,' he said amicably, and drank. Vera watched him with smouldering eyes as he replaced his glass. 'Now,' he said, 'down to business.'

Kate noted with amusement that their table was attracting puzzled glances from all around. She was rather beginning to enjoy the situation—there was something about Uncle Roger's master-strokes, cruel though they might be, that was wickedly, irresistibly funny.

'Did Mr Potter read the will to you?' she asked.

'The will? Oh no, of course not,' replied the priest happily. 'That would have been wrong, no?'

'So you don't know the contents?' put in Vera.

Once again, a puzzled expression had appeared on the priest's open features. 'No, I don't know the contents, of course not. Have I not just said so?'

'But didn't you ask?'

'Ask?' He looked from one to the other. 'That is for Carlo, yes? Not for *me*.'

'Carlo?' A faint glimmer of hope had appeared on Vera's face. 'Which Carlo?'

'Which Carlo?' Father Castelli took a firm grip on the short hair at the back of his grizzled head, and tugged hard. A hunted look crossed his face. 'Carlo Castelli, of course.'

'Then you—you're *not* Carlo Castelli?'

Light dawned suddenly on the priest's face. He threw back his head and barked happily with laughter. Several amused faces turned their way.

'No, no, no, no.' Father Castelli shook a large forefinger in negation. 'I am *Peppino* Castelli, from St Joseph's, here in London. Carlo is my cousin. Now you see? And I have come to tell you that Carlo is delayed, because of fog at Milan airport. But he is on his way now. You see?'

'Tell me, Father,' said Vera de Cruz, 'your cousin Carlo—he isn't married, is he?'

'Oh no,' said the priest, surprised. 'Carlo is a bachelor.'

'Waiter,' called Vera happily, 'bring the father another orange juice. And make mine a double!'

An hour later, having made her excuses, and having promised to visit Father Castelli at his parish some time, Kate slipped out of the hotel and took the Tube back to her little flat near Wimbledon Common. Despite the prestigious address, her flat was a humble enough residence. She had decorated it herself, and the walls were covered with the fine, detailed flower-studies which she loved to paint. After a lean two-year period, Kate Melville's watercolours were beginning to sell. And her work was becoming recognised as amongst the best of its kind. Her botanical studies—birds, butterflies, wild flowers— had begun to fetch good prices in commercial galleries; and Harrods had recently taken a series of autumn landscapes which she had done the year before. With the article—small, it was true, but flattering nonetheless— which had appeared about her in the *Telegraph*, Kate's prospects seemed brighter than they had been for years. It had been a hard struggle, sustained only by the occasional job illustrating children's books or designing calendars; but Kate Melville was no stranger to hardship. Since that appalling day in June, when she was seventeen years old, she had been alone. And after her parents' death had come the news that her father and mother had been living on credit. That they had chosen a very bad moment to die. Because they had left their grief-stricken daughter nothing but debts.

Somehow she had resisted both the charity of the State and the trap of poverty. She had worked her way through 'A' levels, and then through art college. And if the last five years had sobered her, and left her a little more solemn than a twenty-two-year-old girl should be—especially one so pretty and talented as Kate Melville—they had also matured her beyond her years. And they had given her the rare quality of being able to be satisfied with what she had.

As she made herself coffee, and buttered a scone, Kate reflected wryly on the afternoon's events. Uncle Roger's Sicilian island meant little to her. It was a dream-place, something out of her orbit. It was not even worth contemplating. She dismissed Vera de Cruz, Leparú, Uncle Roger, and Carlo Castelli with one thought, picked up her coffee and scone, and carried them over to her workbench. Under the bright Anglepoise lamp, she studied the half-finished painting she been busy with that morning. It showed a collection of dried flowers she had gathered on the Common days earlier. To the ordinary eye, the vase full of flowers would have seemed very ordinary; but Kate had found the hidden colours and shapes, the quiet poetry of the arrangement, that would make the painting a continual delight for whoever would eventually buy it. Without vanity, she recognised that the study was going well. She took out the letter which Sebastian Potter had passed on to her, and opened it.

Inside was a draft for five thousand pounds. Taken aback, she unfolded the letter, and read it.

My dear Caterina,
This cheque is a very small gift for a very dear niece. As you will have heard by now, there are greater prizes yet in store—though you'll have to win those, as they can't be given. You'll see why, one day. Dear Kate, you probably think this is yet another of your eccentric uncle's whims. But you were one of the few people who realised that my jokes always had a deeper purpose. Well, this one's no exception. By now I shall be at rest, my dear niece. Remember me now and then. Au revoir.

There was no signature. Kate's eyes had misted over as she read the note. It was characteristic of Roger Courtney's terse, cryptic style. She reflected sadly that the man's life seemed to have been so unluckily clouded over. Had he been born twenty years later, the tolerant attitudes of a new generation would have made a place for Roger, would even have welcomed his irreverent, mischievous humour. It had been unlucky that he should have been given such a staid age to live in. She laid the letter aside with a sigh, and picking up a large sable brush, began to mix a deep russet red in her paint-tray.

She worked constantly for an hour, bringing the painting to its final state. By the time she was putting in the fine details with a little sharp brush, it was eight-thirty in the evening. Her stomach told her that it was time for a light snack, and she remembered that there was a Humphrey Bogart film on television. She was in the middle of rinsing her brushes in the sink when she heard the sound of her doorbell ringing. And something strange happened. As she dried her hands, on the way to the door, there was the slightest doubt in her mind as to who the caller would be. She opened the door, her heart beating fast, and looked up into the most magnificently beautiful eyes she had ever seen.

'Caterina?' asked a deep voice. 'My name is Carlo Castelli. May I come in?'

CHAPTER TWO

As she let Carlo Castelli in, Kate's mind was spinning. In all her vague thoughts about the mysterious third beneficiary of Roger's will, it had never occurred to her that he would be quite so—so—the only word was *magnificent*. The beautifully-cut and undoubtedly foreign astrakhan coat he wore slung over his shoulders could not disguise the lean, lithe power of his body. His movements were sure, expressing confident power; and it was power, and authority, too, which sat on the stunningly handsome face. Yet it had been his eyes, from the first, which had fascinated Kate. They were holding her now, exploring her face with calm curiosity.

'I—I was about to make some coffee, Signor Castelli.' she ventured. 'May I offer you some?'

'That is very kind.' He slipped the coat off wide shoulders, revealing a charcoal-grey suit of the perfection which only Italian tailors seem to achieve. 'I have spent most of the day caged in a departure lounge, unable to either depart or to lounge.' He smiled, and the grey-green spendour of his eyes jolted Kate squarely in the heart. Her mouth was unaccountably dry as she reached out for his coat. 'May I take that? I'll hang it up for you.' Suddenly, she was very grateful for an excuse to flee from his overwhelmingly male presence into the corridor. The warm astrakhan was faintly, expensively, scented; and as she hung it up, she wondered desperately what it was about that warm grey-green gaze that reduced her to the stammering shyness of a schoolgirl who had never been closer to a man than three feet from a balding geography master!

She came uncertainly back into the room. Carlo Castelli was standing with his back to her, gazing at the paintings on the wall, hands on hips. She had time to notice that his sleek black hair was impeccably cut before he turned to her.

'Your paintings are even finer than I had expected, Caterina.' His voice was deep, his accent faintly foreign. Summoning her poise, she smiled back at him.

'Thank you, Signor Castelli. But who led you to expect that I was a painter?'

'Your uncle,' he said, with a quirk of his splendid, passionate mouth. 'Who else? Roger was very eager to send you money to pay for your painting school. Did you know that?'

'No,' she said, taken aback. 'He never mentioned it.'

'He decided it would be better for you to have to finance your own education.' The dazzling eyes were faintly amused now. 'For such an irresponsible man, Caterina, your uncle had surprisingly old-fashioned ideas about responsibility.'

'Please sit down,' she invited. 'I'll get the coffee in a minute. Have you seen Mr Potter yet?'

'Yes,' he purred, 'I managed to catch Mr Potter just before the clockwork ran down.'

'The clockwork?' she asked, puzzled.

'Oh yes,' he said calmly. 'Mr Potter runs on clockwork. Not flesh and blood, like you or me. All Mr Potters do. Somebody winds them up with a key in the morning, and they run down in the evening, and are put back in the cupboard.'

Despite herself, Kate smiled at his strange image. 'So,' she said, 'you've heard what Uncle Roger's last joke was? I mean the terms of the will.' To her horror, she felt the blood mounting to her cheeks as the words left her mouth.

'Caterina,' he said with laughing eyes, 'you seem to be blushing. Is something the matter?'

'Nothing,' she said, wishing the earth would swallow her there and then. 'I'll get that coffee now.' She fled into the kitchen, cursing the weakness at her knees. What on earth was wrong with her? She had never behaved so gauchely in her life! As she fumbled with the kettle, she examined the face that was indelibly imprinted in her mind's eye. It had the perfection of something sculpted by Michelangelo; yet the golden skin and the cloudy emerald eyes were staggeringly alive. Vitality and authority burned in this man like a flame. And from the hand-made leather shoes and the red silk tie to the beautiful hands and the thick black lashes which helped make those eyes so damnably lovely, Carlo Castelli breathed the sophisticated life and taste of Europe.

Why had all her customary solemn poise left her? Kate was no stranger to handsome men. Her own striking good looks had ensured that there was always a steady queue of young men eager to take her out. And she was something of an expert at fending off their sometimes too pressing attentions. Yet Carlo Castelli had crashed through her defences as though they weren't even there, reducing her to a blushing confusion she thought had been left behind for ever. He was older than most of the boy-friends she had known, yet it was more than that; he projected the complete, arrogant confidence of a man who knew what he wanted, and who was used to getting it.

'Pull yourself together, Kate,' she told herself as she

picked up the tray and carried it through. His eyes met hers with smoky amusement.

'Have you recovered, *cara?*'

'Do you take milk, Signor Castelli?' she asked coolly, setting down the tray.

'Ah, you *have* recovered your poise,' he smiled. 'And no, I don't take milk. Why is it that the English insist on diluting everything—tea, coffee, chocolate—with milk?'

'And sugar?'

'Sugar, yes. Now, sit down, Caterina Melville, and let us talk.' He said her surname with the accent on the second syllable, so that it sounded foreign, French.

'What do you wish to talk about, Signor Castelli?'

'Your mischievous uncle, for one thing,' he smiled. 'And please call me Carlo. So—you are embarrassed by the terms of Roger's will?'

'They don't concern me,' she shrugged, avoiding the splendid eyes.

'Oh, but they do,' he said softly. 'Indubitably. I have not yet met Miss de Cruz—is she Spanish?'

'Half Spanish. Vera is one of my mother's cousins—she was born in Madrid.'

'I see. And what does *she* think about Roger's will?'

'You'll have to ask her yourself,' replied Kate, gulping at her coffee.

'I see,' he drawled again. 'You are not excited by the idea of inheriting Leparú?'

'The whole idea is impossible,' she retorted.

'Impossible?' His lambent eyes met hers with shocking directness, and a slow smile curved the beautiful line of his mouth. 'On the contrary, *cara*, the idea is eminently possible.'

'Speak to Vera, then,' said Kate shortly. 'She seems to think the same way you do.'

'Really?' he asked softly. 'You mean she wants Leparú?'

'She's dying for it. She's been talking the whole afternoon about marrying you, *signor*—and she'll leap into your arms at a word from you. Especially when she sees how—'

'How what?' he purred lazily, the green embers of his eyes watching her face.

Unwillingly, Kate pressed on.

'When she sees that you're not exactly hideous, Signor Castelli, she'll be throwing herself at your feet.'

'Not exactly hideous?' Suddenly he threw up his chin and laughed, a delightful chuckle low in his throat which set Kate's nerve-ends quivering. 'You are scarcely complimentary, *cara!*'

'No doubt you're more used to swooning women,' she retorted. 'Perhaps you've grown too used to compliments?'

'You mean that I am more than—not hideous?' he asked gently, lowering his lashes mockingly over the emerald fire of his eyes. 'Come now! That is a little more flattering. But what about you, my dear Caterina—you are scarcely unused to sweet talk yourself? There must have been dozens of men in your life with charming remarks on their lips about your golden hair, your cornflower eyes, your—' he waved a strong hand elegantly at her body, a wicked humour glinting in his face, '—your lissom endowments. Am I too personal?'

'Men say these things,' she replied, trying to sound calm and mature. 'They like to flatter women, certainly, until they can get their way.'

'Yet something tells me they do not get their way with you, *cara.*' His mouth was mocking.

'What tells you that, *signor?*'

'The little chips of ice in those sapphire eyes. And a certain catlike expression in them.' His smile widened, his lips parting to show beautiful white teeth. 'You are something of an ice-maiden, I think. Am I wrong?'

'I've had a strict life, *signor,*' she replied cooly. 'There hasn't been much time for men. I am an ice-maiden, if you like. But I know what I want.'

'Do you, indeed. And what is that?'

'My career. My art.'

'Ah, yes.' He glanced at the three studies of roses that hung on the wall above her head. 'Your art. And you do not care for male company at all?'

'I don't need it, *signor.*' She met the dazzling amusement of his eyes, trying to still the beating of her heart. 'But why are you so concerned about my attitude towards men?'

'Because fate has thrown us together, Caterina,' he drawled, and she could not tell whether he was mocking or serious. She examined the golden face.

'Fate has not done anything of the sort,' she said. 'I've told you—if you want the island of Leparú, go and speak to Vera. She shares your interest exactly—I'm sure you'll get something sorted out.'

'Do *you* not want the island of Leparú?'

'Not in the slightest,' she replied calmly.

His eyes widened, and their smoky grey-green depths shone like sunlight through a wave. 'Clearly you have never seen Leparú, my dear. It's a little piece of Paradise.'

'I resigned myself to not having Paradise many years ago, *signor.* It will not grieve me to miss it once more.'

'Pah!' He smiled mockingly at her. 'You talk like an old woman—like someone who has done it all, seen everything. How old are you? Twenty-two? Twenty-three? Surely there is red blood in your veins? A little flame in your heart? I do not believe that it has all frozen over!'

'Simply because I don't care for men, and have no urge to possess land, *signor*, it doesn't mean that I'm entirely frozen.'

'Poor little old maid!' He rose from the chair with the grace of a leopard, and stepped over to the painting she had been working on. 'You have made yourself a little winter here. A little igloo of snow and ice, where you closet yourself away with your dried flowers and your pressed leaves, and your paintings of autumn.' He turned to her, all the wicked amusement and life in his body seeming to be concentrated in his eyes. 'Do you know anything about the world, *cara?* I wonder if you can imagine Leparú?'

'One island is very much like another,' she replied, trying to disguise the fact that his words had set a little flame beating at her pulses.

'You are wrong, Caterina Melville.' Suddenly he came over to her, and dropped on to his haunches, his strong hands clasping the arms of the chair she was sitting in. Involuntarily, she shrank back from the magnificently beautiful face that was staring into hers. The throbbing at her pulses had suddenly become a trembling, and she knew that very little was stopping her from leaping out of the chair and running like a hare out of the door and on to the wild safety of Wimbledon Common.

'You cannot imagine what it is like,' he said, his voice full of vitality. 'You have spent too long under grey skies and between damp walls to remember that the sky can be blue. And the sky in Sicily is blue, blue, blue—deep, cobalt blue, that burns down like the eyes of God. The sea is warm under the sun, the beaches are hot and white. The earth is rich, and abundant with life—oranges, lemons, corn, wheat, olives. Do you know why Etna continues to smoke, *cara*?'

She shook her head, dumbly, fascinated by him.

'The ancients said it was because the king of the gods had buried a Titan deep in the earth, and had piled a mountain on him to pin him there. And when he struggles deep under the ground, flames and molten rock burst from the peak above. There is life even in the savage depths of the volcano, Caterina.' The splendid eyes were holding hers so intently that Kate was beginning to feel faint. The blood was rushing in her ears, and in a minute, she was going to slip forward against him . . .

'As for Leparú,' he said, standing up, 'can you imagine a giant hand, casting a handful of jewels into the sea? One of them is Leparú. It is covered with wild olive-trees, with cycads, and palms. And Roger, poor eccentric Roger, has built a palace there. For you, *cara*. It is within your grasp. Do you still tell me you are indifferent to it?'

'It doesn't tempt me,' she repeated, watching the cat-like grace of his movements.

'It doesn't tempt you,' he repeated mockingly. 'Does it not strike you as significant that you—a virgin—should despise men? That you—an ice-maiden—should dread the fire?'

'Are you suggesting I should marry you, simply to inherit Leparú?' A dangerous light danced in his eyes.

'If you married me,' he snarled, 'you would gain infinitely more than Leparú.'

'What would I gain, *signor*?'

'Life. All the million things that go up to make life—and not this half-death you have here.'

'Tell me one of the millions of things,' she asked trying to preserve her cool exterior.

'For one thing,' he smiled, the silvery emeralds of his eyes meeting hers with heart-stopping concentration, 'you would gain the shuddering ecstasy of love.'

His directness took her breath away. 'You don't mince your words, *signor*,' she gasped. 'And you're very arrogant!'

'Not arrogant,' he answered, a wicked smile curving those beautiful, eminently kissable lips, 'just confident.'

Kate's heart was still shaken by what he had said—and how he had looked. 'It doesn't occur to you,' she retorted coldly, 'that there are some women who can do very well without men?'

'Yes?' he drawled. 'And are there some plants which do very well without sun?'

'There are, as a matter of fact,' she replied triumphantly.

'Oh, I had forgotten.' The low, delicious laugh gurgled in his throat again. 'There are mosses and lichens, are there not? And certain kinds of rare fungus. But you are not one of those! With your bright blue eyes, and your sweet face, you could have been a mermaid or a sea-nymph, swimming in the Mediterranean foam. Can a woman with the colour of the summer sky in her eyes really be happy living out of the sun?'

Angrily Kate avoided his eyes. Her thoughts about love had always been shy, intimate. The thought of surrendering herself to the possession of a man had always alarmed her; she shrank from the physicality of love, dreading the ruthless invasion of her inmost secrets that a wilful man would surely desire. As though he had read her thoughts with uncanny accuracy, Carlo Castelli sat on the stool next to her, leaning on the arm of her chair, and met her eyes with mocking gentleness.

'You are afraid, little mermaid, are you not? You are terrified of the boisterous waves! You think they will smash all your illusions flat, crush the life out of you!'

'Isn't that what love means, in real life?'

'Is it? Are you such an expert on love?'

'Are you, *signor*?' She met the challenge of his magnificent eyes unflinchingly. 'I have no desire to test the truth of my convictions. I choose to be an ice-maiden because I love my art. I cannot love anyone who will take me away from my art.'

'Your art? Your little brushes, your tiny tubes of paint, your stumps of pencil? Do you think love would diminish your power to interpret life through your painting? Ah, you are mistaken, *cara*!' He shook his head at her. 'Listen to me. My grandmother was a singer—a soprano *coloratura*, who sang before King Victor Emmanuel himself. When she was your age, she was the toast of all Italy. Yet it was said that her voice was never so sweet, so true, as it was after she married my grandfather. And then, they say, she sang like an angel!'

Kate stood up abruptly. 'Would you like some more coffee?' she asked, pouring herself another cup. He shook his head, and she walked away from him to the window to draw the curtains. Her reflection in the dark glass met her eyes as she reached out for the curtains. Without turning around, she said, 'Signor Castelli, let's leave the subject of marriage alone for a while.'

'But of course,' he purred. 'It was you, and not I, who brought it up.'

She drew the curtains, and turned to face him. 'But you were the one who brought the subject up, *signor*. It was you who suggested marrying me as a way of getting—'

'Marrying you?' The bold mouth curved into a smile that was utterly mocking. 'You don't dream that I've just been proposing to you, surely?'

'But—'

'For an ice-maiden, you are remarkably quick to hear talk of marriage, my dear Caterina,' he drawled. The long lashes were lowered over his eyes again, and the strong, amused face registered mock-surprise. 'I assure you, *cara*, that if I were to propose to you, I would make myself absolutely clear. And I am not in the habit of proposing to every stranger I meet.'

'I thought fate had thrown us together?' she asked, the blood hot in her cheeks. He had made her look a complete fool, and she was fuming inwardly. 'I suppose you're laughing at me now?'

'Not at all,' he drawled. 'I am merely surprised that you should think my intentions so honourable.'

'Why—did you come here to seduce me, *signor*?' she asked ironically.

The emerald eyes flattered her figure with a smoky, amused gaze. '*Cara*—if, as you say, Vera de Cruz is perfectly willing to marry me, then why should I be here at all?'

'I've no idea,' she said shortly. 'Why don't you go and look her up right now? Maybe you can persuade your cousin Peppino to marry the two of you tomorrow!'

He chuckled softly. 'I scarcely think so, ice-maiden. Peppino is a good priest—he would never consent to marry anyone for purely mercenary considerations. But there is something in what you say. Is your relation as pretty as you are?'

'Much prettier,' said Kate angrily. 'And she's a good eight years older, too.'

'Do I detect a note of jealousy in your voice?' he enquired, his eyes opening wide.

'Not at all. In fact, I think Vera would suit you down to the ground. She's just your type. And she's half Spanish—perhaps she will respond better to the idea of Mediterranean delights than a plain little Englishwoman like me.'

'No, not plain,' he said softly. 'Your face is like a rose, and your body is as light and as supple as a dancer's.' His lips parted to show his sharp, straight teeth again. 'You would make a desirable partner for any man, little ice-maiden.'

'Any man who didn't value his eyes,' snapped Kate.

'Yes—you would probably scratch like a wildcat. It would be like taking a snow-leopard.' The flickering light in the silvery-green eyes was like copper burning, and his tongue touched his white teeth for a second, as though he were actually contemplating the taste of her. Kate set her chin up, trying not to let her mouth tremble, and his dark eyebrows lifted slightly.

'Are you alarmed at something?'

'Not at all,' she rejoined. 'Why is it that men like the idea of taking a woman by force, *signor*? Do they enjoy the idea of inflicting pain? Of being scratched and bitten themselves?'

'The thought of being scratched and bitten does not please *me*, I assure you. My women always co-operate.' The smile that touched his face revealed with utter clarity the powerful, untamed spirit within the magnificent body. 'Although,' he added, his eyes on hers, 'some of them have certainly scratched and bitten—at certain passionate moments!'

'You go too far!' she gasped. 'Go and tell all this to Vera de Cruz, Signor Castelli—she at least will enjoy it!'

He considered her calmly. 'Yes,' he said, 'you are Roger Courtney's niece all right. You have the same quick temper. Roger was very fond of you, Caterina. Did you know that?'

'I was the only member of the family who bothered to write to him,' she shrugged, still affronted at the directness of his speech.

'Yes,' he nodded. 'It meant a lot to him.' He glanced around the walls of the little sitting-room. 'Roger used to show me your letters. He was so proud of you. Every time we met, he would have another one to show me—delightful letters, Caterina, so full of wisdom and wit. And all the little drawings in the margins, and sometimes pressed flowers.' He smiled, gently this time. Kate was profoundly disturbed at the thought that this glamorous, mocking stranger had read her unguarded letters; letters that she knew would have told the story of how one lonely girl had grown from innocent immaturity to determined adulthood.

'I'm glad you enjoyed them,' she said tonelessly.

'Are you offended?'

'There was nothing in those letters to be ashamed of. No doubt you had many a good chuckle over them.'

'That's not fair,' he said softly. 'I told you, they were delightful letters. All they showed me was the quick mind of a maturing woman.'

'Tell me, Signor Castelli,' Kate said, 'have you any idea why Roger should have made this extraordinary will? How did you come to know him?'

'Through my cousin,' he replied. 'Did your uncle ever mention Lidia in his letters?'

'No,' she said, intrigued.

He nodded. 'Your uncle was a good man, Caterina. Strange and undisciplined, even wild; but when he loved, he loved deeply and well. It was simply his misfortune in life to love the wrong women.'

'You mean your cousin didn't love him in return?'

'Lidia is happily married, with two children. Yet she understood Roger. There was a suffering quality beneath his flippant exterior which touched Lydia's heart. She and Giacomo were regular visitors at Leparú. His love for Lidia was one more thing which drove him into himself.'

'He spoke of you now and then, Signor Castelli,' she said, suddenly strangely shy. 'He told me you were a good friend to him.'

'He was older than I, of course; but yes, we were good friends.' The beautiful eyes were dark now, as dark as a winter sea. 'Your uncle had become so accustomed to hiding his suffering, Caterina, that it was second nature to him. He never mentioned the appalling pains in his side, until it was too late. When the cancer was finally diagnosed, it was inoperable. When you come to Sicily, we shall go and visit his grave at Catania.' His last words shook Kate suddenly out of the sombre mood that had fallen over her.

'When I come to Sicily?' she asked. 'I'm not coming to Sicily, *signor!*'

'Oh, but I think you will,' he smiled, his eyes lazy on her face. 'In any case, we can discuss it over dinner tomorrow.'

'Dinner tomorrow?'

'You sound like Echo answering poor Narcissus, Caterina. Yes, tomorrow. We are having dinner together.' He glanced at his watch, a wafer-thin gold Cartier that looked somehow fragile against the sinewy strength of his wrist. 'It's getting late, and I am tired. When I come to London, I stay at my club, the St James', in Regent Street.' He rose with characteristic fluid grace. 'Shall we say about eight?"

'You take my breath away, Signor Castelli,' Kate told him. 'I have no desire to eat with you in some stuffy old club at all!'

'The sweetest faces make the best liars,' he said. 'You will be there, *cara*. I would stake my life on it.' He smiled wickedly, beautifully. 'May I have my coat back, please?'

'It's the strangest thing I've ever heard,' said Beth Hussey. She picked up Kate's plate, and disappeared into the kitchen with it to fetch the puddings. 'And you say he's an attractive man?' she called, head in the fridge. An old friend from art school, Beth had long been the recipient of Kate's confidences. Her gamine face and bizarre sense of dress concealed a quick and sympathetic mind, and where most people were inclined to dismiss her as slightly mad, with her orange-dyed hair and her flowing hand-printed dresses, Kate had come to value her friend's intelligent advice. It was usually worth the ordeal of Beth's erratic and sometimes horrific cooking to get the benefit of her thoughts on any problem. Which was why Kate had come to see Beth the next day, after a somewhat troubled morning at her desk.

'Yes,' she answered, 'he's very attractive. Black hair, grey-green eyes, built like Apollo—you know the type.'

'I very much regret to say I don't,' grinned Beth, bringing two little bowls to the table. 'My men are usually too fat, or too short, or too something. This is banana and gooseberry ice-cream—I made it myself. I hope you like it.'

Kate crunched the frozen, vinegary concoction, and managed to suppress a shudder.

'It's very interesting,' she said diplomatically. 'Very sophisticated. Yes, Carlo's certainly attractive, Beth. But he's not that sort of attractive—he's not ordinary in any way. He frightens me, to tell you the truth. He's as handsome as the devil, and he talks like Don Juan come to life. He's the sort of man you dream about, but would run a mile from if you actually met. There's something ruthless about him—he looks as if he could be quite cruel in getting his way with a woman.'

'He sounds dreadful,' giggled Beth, but the light in her brown eyes showed that she had found Kate's description of Carlo Castelli exciting as well as daunting. 'You're not exactly used to that kind of man, are you, Kate?'

'What do you mean?' asked Kate, slightly offended.

'Well, I know there's always someone ringing up to take you out; but they tend to be so similar, don't they? What my mother would call 'nice boys', with nice manners and nice intentions. From what you say, this Carlo Castelli sounds something of a professional ladykiller. I wonder whether he's not just a little too much for you?'

'I'm not *that* much of an innocent, Beth,' Kate said somewhat shortly.

'Oh, come on, Kate!' Beth waved her spoon reprovingly. 'You've barely been kissed, and you know it.'

There was truth in what Beth was saying. Apart from a few "nice" goodnight pecks, Kate's lips had scarcely known the touch of a man's. While Beth, she knew, was no stranger to love. She had followed one or two of Beth's passionate, dramatic affairs with a mixture of amusement and horror over the years.

'The fact that I've barely been kissed doesn't mean that I'm going to let myself be seduced now.' She finished her gritty ice-cream with relief, and pushed her bowl away. 'I think I can take care of myself.'

'Well, don't forget that Signor Castelli has two very good reasons for wanting to get his way with you, Katherine.'

'What are they?'

'For one thing,' Beth replied, smiling gently at her, 'you're rather delightful, in an innocent sort of way. You probably never knew it, but half the class at art school was in love with you, Kate. Your eyes are a very deep blue— it's quite unusual —and you've got that sort of face and figure that sets nice young men thinking about wedding-bells and diamond rings. It would definitely set a not-so-nice young man thinking of champagne, roses, and seduction.'

'I'm not sure whether to be alarmed or flattered,' Kate said flippantly.

Beth pursed her pink mouth judiciously. 'In this case, I'd definitely be alarmed, old chum. Besides, there's something about virginal innocence which is like a red rag to a bull with these Casanova types. Remember what they said about Don Giovanni? He had a passion for maidens.'

'And the second reason?'

'Leparú,' said Beth succinctly. 'Remember that Signor Castelli can't get his hands on the place without a marriage licence. And if he can make you fall in love with him, and hustle you into marrying him, he'll end up a very rich man.'

'He didn't strike me as exactly poverty-stricken,' said

Kate thoughtfully. 'His clothes are beautiful—and he's got that sort of atmosphere about him, of someone who always gets the very best.'

'Which is a good reason for him needing a bit of ready cash,' retorted Beth. 'And it rather looks as though you're his key to a quarter of a million.'

'Don't forget Vera, though. If he's that keen on Leparú, Vera's dead keen to oblige him, you know.'

'Hmm. I've met Vera once or twice, Kate. And if I were a man, I'd think very carefully before taking her on.'

'Why? She's only thirty, and she's very good-looking.'

'Listen, you and Vera are like a diamond and a garnet, Kate. At a casual glance, you're just as beautiful, just as precious. But take a second look, and there's no comparison at all. And Vera's got a vicious temper, which won't exactly endear her to a man who likes his freedom.'

Kate sighed, and looked around Beth's cluttered, crazily-furnished house. 'You talk as though Carlo was looking for a partner for life,' she said. 'All he needs is a quick marriage, which can be annulled as soon as possible, leaving him the lion's share of the estate.'

'I'm not sure of that.' Beth took the plates off the table, and Kate followed her into the kitchen to help with the washing up.

'You're a very nice piece of real estate yourself,' Beth continued, switching on the kettle. 'I wonder if it occurs to you that your dear old Uncle Roger has left *you* to Signor Castelli in his will. It's a very nice package—paradisal island with free gorgeous wife thrown in.'

There was a pause while the kettle began to rumble. Kate watched Beth as she busied herself with the teapot, her orange hair falling in her eyes, extravagant green earrings bobbing. There was a lot of hard truth in what

Beth had said so flippantly. And she *did* doubt her ability to fend Carlo Castelli off. After he had left the night before, she had gone straight to bed; and that damnably beautiful face had appeared in her dreams—delicious, confused dreams that she had refused even to remember in the morning. Yet she was wise enough to realise that, cool though her mind might be, Carlo's specifically male appeal was something which transcended her ability to think. His passionate, poetic words to her haunted her still; and she recognised that here was a man as utterly different from her usual English boy-friends as a grown male leopard from a handful of house-trained cats.

Sipping her coffee in Beth's plant-filled sitting-room, Kate was struck once again by the wicked, mischievous humour which had typified Roger Courtney's actions. Bringing Carlo, herself, and Vera together had been the sort of ridiculous cocktail he loved. And for all her suave exterior, Kate knew that Vera was no match for Carlo Castelli. Would he approach Vera? she wondered. He was probably making love to her even now, flattering her with those dazzling, penetrating eyes. She shook the thought away resentfully.

'Are you going to go?' asked Beth.

'Where to?'

'Out to dinner with Signor Castelli. At his club.'

'I don't know,' Kate said truthfully. 'The prospect is slightly intimidating. And these places are very much male preserves, you know. They're all old oak panelling and port-stained butlers. Daddy used to belong to one, and it always made me feel funny, going there.'

'It does have a faintly decayed romance about it, though.' Beth grinned mischievously. 'You could go in a see-through blouse, and give the oldest member heart failure.'

'No, thank you—I'm not giving Carlo any more encouragement than he needs. What do you think?'

'Oh, there's no doubt about it—you *must* go!'

'Must I? I thought you were warning me off a few moments ago?'

'Sure I was. But this is the opportunity of a life time. There's a chance to be seduced by a real expert, Kate, and you can't possibly pass it up.'

'Beth!'

'I mean it,' she smiled. 'Every woman deserves one night of bliss. And by my reckoning, you're allowed at least ten indiscretions in your life, before you settle down to marriage and the propagation of the species. If Carlo Castelli turns out a scoundrel, then at least you'll have one magnificent memory to warm yourself with in your old age! And if he's not—well, who knows?'

'I've always suspected you of being immoral,' Kate rejoined, shaking her blonde head, 'but now I know it.'

'There's not much he can do in the St James' Club, Kate. And if you're so sure you can handle yourself, why don't you let him have a good crack at you.'

'*A good crack?*' Kate repeated, laughing. 'You're a born romantic, Beth. I've never heard it put so subtly!'

'It will be an education to see a real Casanova in action, anyway. Look—the food at the St James' is wonderful, so I've heard. And it's a lovely place. And if Signor Castelli is all you've made him out to be, it ought to be an evening to remember. You can just look on coolly, while he covers your white hand with hot kisses—you know, like in the old movies.'

'But this won't be an old movie—this will be for real.'

'*Naturellement, chérie!*' Beth put on her Charles Aznavour voice. 'You and ze muzeek, tra-la tra-la, dancing wiz you . . .'

'Come on, Beth,' grinned Kate, 'the coffee's gone to your head. Let's hear about this offer you've had from the Karsh Gallery. I'm going to forget about Carlo and the St James' until the very last minute—and then I'll toss a coin!'

CHAPTER THREE

THE commissionaire was a splendid old gentleman in a navy blue uniform, with the medals of a dozen different campaigns glinting on his manly breast. He saluted with an admirable mixture of gallantry and military precision as he opened the door of her cab. The rain that was spattering on the beautiful canvas awning over the gold and mahogany entrance to the eighteenth century club also made soft wet dents in the silver fur that Kate had wrapped over the pale silk of her dress. She had been determined to show Carlo that, ice-maiden though she might be, she was capable of dressing up to the requirements of the St James'. She knew that the forget-me-not blue of the silk had set shimmering lights in her own almost violet eyes; and the only jewellery she wore, the diamonds that sparkled in her ears, perfectly set off the rather cool beauty of the ensemble. She felt confident, slightly excited. And the way that the commissionaire ran a gloved finger under his grey moustache, recalling the appreciative chivalry of a bygone age, told her that she was looking as good as she felt.

'Was you meeting one of the gentlemen, miss?' he asked as he ushered her to the discreetly-lit entrance of the club.

'Yes, I was,' she said. 'I believe he's just arrived from Italy—Signor Castelli.'

'Don't you worry, miss—*I* know Signor Castelli. Proper gent, if I may make so bold. Would you mind waiting in the entrance hall while I fetch him? Club's rules, I'm afraid, miss.'

Kate looked curiously around the foyer as she waited. The generous, noble proportions of the eighteenth century lent the room a spacious sense of dignity. The gleaming wood of the ceiling, the panelling, and the ornate reception-desk had been intricately carved. The carpet was a deep, rich red, and on one wall, above the velvet-covered sofa, a huge painting of the battle of Waterloo dominated the room. The smell of cigar-smoke that wafted discreetly from the rooms beyond completed the picture of absolute male dominance. This foyer was like the entrance to another world, two hundred years away from the twentieth century and all its ugly, sordid bustle. This was a world where women's rights had not even been discussed yet, where the moon was still chaste and untrodden by man's foot, where one rode in carriages or barouches. In its way, it was utterly seductive; though its arrogance made a few of Kate's hackles stand on end.

She was just deciding that the vast mirror which flanked the curtained doorway was faintly pink-tinted, when the dark curtain itself was thrown aside, and Carlo Castelli strode out towards her, accompanied by his beautiful reflection. She could not prevent her heart from quivering at the sight of him, but she was confident in her own beauty tonight, and she stretched out a cool hand to greet him. He took it in his own, and brushed it with his lips, seeming to leave a little flame on her skin. Then, still holding her slender fingers, he smiled into her eyes.

'You are very beautiful,' he said softly. 'I am glad you chose to be here tonight.'

She met the warm intoxication of his eyes boldly.

'Did you have any doubts, *signor?*'

'I would have staked my life on your presence here,' he purred. 'Did I not say so? But when are you going to begin calling me by my first name?'

She glanced at the curving smile on the wonderful, sensuous mouth, then raised her eyes to meet his again.

'I think I must reserve that intimacy for better acquaintance, Signor Castelli,' she said calmly.

He bowed, the sultry emerald light in his eyes hidden beneath mocking lashes. Then he took her by the arms, and spun her lightly, so that they were looking at their own reflections in the pink-tinged mirror.

'Look,' he said, 'is that not a handsome couple?'

She looked at the glamorous image, fascinated for an instant. Carlo was splendid, authoritative, in dark and faultless evening dress, the single red rose at his lapel setting off the severe black-and-white of suit and shirt. Beside his lean, powerful figure, her own was slight, a thistledown-airy maiden, made of snow and sky-stained frost. She looked up into the golden face of the man next to her, a smile touching her lips.

'You're vain, *signor!* It doesn't please all women to look at themselves.'

'Come, then,' he smiled, walking her to the dark curtain. 'Have you ever been in the St James' before?'

'Never. But my father had a club when he was alive, and I was taken there now and then as a special treat.'

'By the expression on your face, the treat was not so special?'

'To tell the truth, it was somewhat boring for a little girl. Although I look forward to visiting this particular bastion of male chauvinism. I would have thought these places were a thing of the past.'

'Oh, but they are,' he said. He held the curtain aside for her. 'Welcome to the past, Caterina.'

The wide sitting-room, with its leather arm-chairs, its racks of beautiful old firearms and antique swords, its oil-paintings of glossy horses and smoky battle scenes and storm-tossed ships, met Kate's gaze like a scene come to life from an eighteenth century novel. The Regency gilding on the alcoves and the flowered patterning in the walnut panels added a touch of richness to the severity of the room. Carlo leaned gracefully against the cold, rounded white buttock of a marble Venus to study her reaction. Kate was entranced.

'This is like something out of a period film,' she exclaimed softly.

'It is unique,' he nodded. 'Do you like it?'

'It's not exactly designed to please the female eye,' she smiled. 'And it smells far too much of leather and cigars and—' she sniffed the air appreciatively, '—and gunpowder and sea-spray and wet horses to please the female taste. But it is, as you say, *signor*, unique.'

'But we will not stay here—I do not intend to share you with the covetous eyes of the other members to-night.' He led her through the long room into another small hallway where a spectacular Victorian staircase led up to further rooms beyond.

'Where are you leading me?' she asked slightly nervously.

'To Bluebeard's chamber,' he said, the mock-ferocity of his lowered black brows all too alarming to Kate.

'Is that where the bodies of all your other women are preserved?' she answered lightly.

He shook his head. 'I am more discreet than that, *cara* — my victims are better hidden.'

'Do you bury them, then?'

'Come,' he said, stopping halfway up the stairs, and turning to her with lambent eyes, 'let us have no more talk of death tonight. I wish to bring you life, Caterina. Remember that.' The sharp white teeth glinted beautifully between his lips as he smiled, and led her to the top of the stairs.

A white-coated waiter was waiting for them at the doorway to a room.

'Good evening, Signor Castelli. Good evening, madame. Everything is ready—won't you please come this way?' He ushered them into the room, and once again Kate had the strange sensation of stepping into another world. She could not suppress a little gasp of pleasure. The oval breakfast-table had been laid for two. But it had been laid for two princes, two lovers, with crystal and white linen, with the soft glow of antique silver and the freshness of rosebuds. The room was quite small, and the atmosphere in it was utterly different from the male robustness of the decor below. This was a room made for a woman's taste. The peaches and maroons of the Turkish rug on the floor were picked up by the salmon pinks of the delightful flower study on one wall. The furniture was delicate and graceful, and the chandelier which hung over the table glittered like a frozen fountain of diamonds. Carlo's firm hand at the back of her waist guided her into the joyous perfection of the little dining-room. She turned to him, eyes shining.

'When you asked me to dine with you, Carlo, I hardly expected this!'

He smiled urbanely. 'I do not know what pleases me more,' he purred, 'the pleasure in your delightful eyes, or the fact that you have at last consented to call me Carlo.'

Confused, Kate shook her head.

'Did I call you that? I don't remember, *signor*. It may have been a slip of the tongue. But this room is very lovely!' She allowed him to guide her into her chair, surrendering her fur to him as she did so. His eyes dropped to her creamy shoulders with unmistakable pleasure, lingering with calm, deliberate interest at her décolletage.

'I was wrong, my dear Caterina—you are no ice-maiden. You are a positive snow queen.' He passed her wrap to the attending waiter, and seated himself opposite her. It occurred to Kate for the first time that she was going to have to spend the entire meal face to face with Carlo Castelli, and her heart quickened nervously at the thought. It was difficult enough to meet those panther's eyes at the best of times. But to be imprisoned here in this luxurious, slightly sensual room with no escape from their penetrating gaze would be an ordeal—a test. She dropped her own eyes from his, feeling the colour touch her cheeks slightly, and toyed idly with the glittering stem of the crystal goblet.

'So this is Bluebeard's chamber,' she murmured. 'How many women have you taken here, *signor*?'

'You are the first, of course,' he said, but the teasing lilt in his voice made her look up and catch the amusement in the bold face.

'Tell me,' she said, 'how have you spent the day?'

'Are you so curious about me, *cara*?'

'My bet is that you spent the day with a relation of mine—Vera de Cruz. Am I correct?' He ignored her question. 'I have taken the liberty of ordering the menu in advance,' he said. 'I hope you are not offended? I think you will enjoy the meal.'

'Don't evade the question,' she said lightly. 'Have you been to see Vera yet?'

'You must not press me,' he said gently. Yet for all the softness of his tone, there was a velvety authority in his voice that took some of the high colour out of her cheeks as swiftly as an icy breeze. It would be quite wrong, she realised suddenly, to play any games with this man. Roué and rake he might be, but there was power beneath the caressing manner, a blade of steel within the beautiful exterior.

'I did not wish to rebuke you,' he said quietly. 'Now let us enjoy our meal together in peace. *D'accordo?*'

'Agreed,' she replied. Yet the glimpse of the master's steel fist inside the velvet glove had sobered her considerably. It had been merely a tiny moment, yet enough to warn her that this heart-stopping game could have terrible consequences. The whiff of grapeshot she had caught in the air in the dark-panelled rooms down below had been prophetic.

'In honour of an ice-maiden,' he purred, the eyes warm and smiling again, 'I have ordered caviare on cracked ice to begin with— and Russian vodka. Do you approve?'

'Vodka? To begin a meal?'

'Why not?' The waiter laid the great silver platter between them, and the cool breath off the ice touched Kate's cheeks as Carlo leaned forward to take her plate. 'When I was a child,' he said, as he piled the pearly grey granules of the precious food on to her plate, 'My grandmother used to fascinate me for hours with tales of Russia. Take some toast. She sang before the Imperial Court— think of that. And the decadent princes themselves drank champagne from her slipper, and toasted her in iced vodka.'

'Really?' Kate asked, intrigued by the image. She bit into the salty morsel, savouring its marine deliciousness.

'She met Rasputin several times—a wild man, with tormented, wild eyes and a long filthy beard that hung to his waist. The last days of the *ancien régime* were strange and fascinating, my dear Caterina. It was the end of an epoch, the slow disintegration of time's monument. My grandmother could tell such tales, enough to set a young boy's mind aflame!' The grey-green eyes reached into the past for a few seconds, and Kate tried to see the boy he must have been, but was unable. He took the vodka bottle off the trolley, and filled the heavy shot-glasses with the colourless liquor.

'What about your parents?' she ventured.

The corners of his eyes slanted downwards in mock deprecation.

'Alas,' he drawled, 'I was a poor orphan, like you. My mother was a Sicilian witch, and my father was a Roman prince, and one day she stole to his bed, and charmed him to an endless sleep, and rode away with him on the sails of a hurricane.'

Kate's mouth dropped open. 'Are you serious?' she asked stupidly.

The smile that touched his passionate mouth was little more than a quirk of each sharp corner, but his eyes were solemn.

'That is what my grandmother told me, at least.' He raised the glass to her, meeting her eyes with a demonic glint of emerald light. 'To you, *cara*.' Then he tossed the vodka back in one swift movement. Kate followed suit, the fire of the alcohol racing down her throat like molten lava, making her cough a little.

'*Brava!*' he cried ironically, dabbing his mouth with the

snow-white napkin. 'As for myself,' he continued, 'I believed her for many years. But eventually I came to the conclusion that the truth was a little more prosaic. A prince my father certainly was, for my grandfather was of the blood royal. *He* perished in the Great War, before my father was yet out of his mother's womb. As for my mother, she was a Sicilian witch in the sense of possessing a spellbinding beauty. The people of Sicily are not like other people,' he added, smiling wickedly into Kate's fascinated eyes. 'Sometimes their skin is almost black, and sometimes their eyes are like green fire—for the Moors conquered Sicily in the eleventh century, before the Normans drove them out, and now and then the savage Moorish strain resurfaces here and there.'

'Hence your mother's magical powers?' Kate asked.

'So it seems,' he shrugged. 'But my mother was a commoner—worse than a commoner, merely a peasant girl, who smelled of wild basil and almond blossom, and the marriage was clearly impossible. So they ran away together, and hid in the mountains, possessed merely of their youth, their beauty, and their love.' He refilled her glass before she could protest.

'What happened to them?' she asked, absorbed.

He shook his head solemnly, his black brows lowering over the clouded emeralds of his eyes. 'Tragedy overtook them. My father died up there, and my mother had only strength enough to bring their baby to my unforgiving grandmother before she, too, passed into the night.'

'So your grandmother brought you up?'

'Like the she-wolf who suckled the orphans of Rome, yes. But tell me about yourself, Caterina. Your parents were killed when you were seventeen, not so? That must have been very bitter.'

Kate told him the brief, sad story of her parents' death and her own growing up, staring down into the glittering, empty depths of the heavy crystal goblet that she was turning in her fingers. Carlo listened in silence until she had finished, and then pressed the bell to summon the waiter. 'It's not nearly as glamorous as your story,' she concluded lamely, feeling that she had been unable to communicate, in her tongue-tied English way.

'Glamorous? No, Caterina. But an impressive story nonetheless. Perhaps I will tell you what I think of it later. But now, enough of the past for the time being. Did you enjoy your caviare?'

'It was delicious,' she said truthfully. 'You seem to have a talent for getting ths best of everything.'

'I have always refused to settle for less,' he shrugged calmly. 'Life is too short to be satisfied with mediocrity.'

'Yet the best is not cheap, *signor*,' she probed delicately. 'Does the fact that you are the son of a prince mean that you have a prince's estate?'

'It means that I am a prince myself,' he replied, meeting her eyes with a glint of irony.

'Then I should call you—?'

'*Vostra altezza* would be the correct form,' he told her gently, 'if we were living in the past. But Italy is a republic now, and the King is long dead. These titles are of the past, *cara*, as dead as our parents, or last year's almond blossom.'

'Have you no hankering for that past?'

'As an amusement alone. I belong to the present, Caterina—the past is simply a hobby with me, not an obsession.' He watched the waiter wheel in the trolley with its fragrant burden of silver chafing-dishes and its bottle of champagne, dewed with condensation in the ornate ice-bucket.

'You should be flattered tonight,' he told her. 'Mr Perkins is favouring you with some of the Club's finest old silver.'

The elderly waiter smiled serenely; like the commissionaire, he too had a military look about him.

'There are members and members, miss,' he told her with a wink. 'And some of 'em ain't too particular whether they eat off a tin tray or the Regency silver.' He began to serve her with steaming *petits pois*. 'When it comes to Signor Castelli, it's different. And when Signor Castelli remarked as 'ow he was having a special guest to dinner in the Nelson Room, I started polishing the Regency silver.'

By the sparkle in his eye, Kate suddenly realised that he believed her to be Carlo's latest mistress! The colour rose to her cheeks. No doubt it would be all over the club by now. Anger stirred her, and she leaned forward.

'Mr Perkins,' she said firmly, 'Signor Castelli and I are friends, and nothing more. I hope you understand that?'

'Of course, miss,' replied the waiter, raising discreet eyebrows, and moving over to serve Carlo. 'What else should you be? New potatoes, sir? They're fresh today. Now don't you worry, miss,' he continued to Kate, 'not a breath of this will get out. Not from old Colour-Sergeant Perkins, miss.' With a reassuring wink that raised Kate's blood to boiling point, Perkins bowed himself out, and she turned indignantly to Carlo.

'What does he mean, not a word will get out? And why is this called the Nelson Room?'

His bright eyes on her were the eyes of a duellist confronting an adversary.

'Once again the past rises to haunt us,' he smiled. 'It is

said that Nelson brought his aristocratic *inamorata* to this little chamber once, to conceal her from the jealous eyes of her cuckolded husband. Off the little doorway,' he said, gesturing to a recessed door she had not noticed, 'lies another room—a *boudoir*, where, it is said, replete with strawberries and clotted cream, the great soldier and his illicit mistress retired to consummate their passion.'

'Venus and Mars,' retorted Kate angrily. 'So this is where all the little affairs of the St James' are conducted, then?'

He inclined his head with a mocking smile. 'If you wish to put it that way, *cara* . . . But you must eat your lobster before it gets too cold. Let me help you.' With an implement like a silver nutcracker, he snapped the scarlet claws open to reveal the tender white meat within, and poured a generous quantity of the hot butter sauce on to her plate. 'If I were you,' he said gently, 'I would dispense with your knife and fork to eat the lobster—there are occasions when to be over-civilised means to miss out on the best things of life.'

But Kate was still burning with indignation.

'That's why you brought me here, isn't it? To try and compromise me?'

'Why should I wish to do such a thing?' he asked calmly, stripping the white flesh from the shell with practised fingers.

'You know why!' Resentfully she dipped a chunk of lobster into the hot sauce. Carlo's eyes watched her pop the delicious morsel into her mouth, and then met hers with an ironic lift of one eyebrow. 'You are determined to make me a devil, are you not?'

'You are surely no saint, Vostra Altezza,' she retorted bitterly. 'No saint ever had such eyes as yours. The green fire in them belies your smooth words. Is that also a gift from your mother?'

'Like my forked tongue and my cloven hoof,' he agreed drily. 'Yet it is said that women cannot resist a devil, my dear Caterina. They burn with curiosity to see whether the left foot is truly cloven, to touch the tongue and tell whether it is like a serpent's or not.' He showed her a pink, dagger-shaped tongue like a leopard's for a second, then raised the champagne-bottle from its bed of ice, and twisted the mushroom-shaped cork out with a resounding *pop*. 'Perkins has been digging deep into the Club's cellars for us. This is a vintage champagne, pure bottled summer.'

The amber wine foamed and bubbled in the deep goblet as he poured. He clashed his glass against hers and raised it high, his eyes holding hers in a silent toast. They drank, and Kate turned without speaking to her lobster. The meal was utterly delicious, and by the time she was rinsing her butter-coated fingers in the finger-bowls on whose surfaces drifted rose-petals, some of her poise had returned. The pudding Carlo had ordered was a fresh fruit trifle, so redolent with Madeira and cream that it made her head swim. The alcohol she had consumed had set a little fire swimming along her veins. She met his eyes boldly as he refilled her glass at the end of the meal.

'This must have cost a fortune, Signor Castelli. I hope it will have been worth it to you.'

'You talk like a stockbroker's wife,' he mocked. 'But of course, you are no one's wife, are you? How different you are from Nelson's Lady Hamilton, *cara*. That one was a creature of the flesh, voluptuous and all too womanly. While you—you are a being of snow and ice, *non è vero?* No man touches you, though you touch all men's hearts.'

Involuntarily, her eyes flickered to the recessed doorway that led to the love-chamber beyond. He caught the quick glance, and his soft laugh was like a purr of some great cat. 'What could possibly melt the snow-queen's mantle, eh, Caterina? Surely not a mere devil with a green flame in his eyes?'

The ex-sergeant brought a rich-smelling ewer of coffee for them, and Carlo leaned back in his seat to watch. 'Have you enjoyed your food?' he asked softly.

'It was very good,' Kate said shortly. 'What have you planned for the rest of the evening, Prince Carlo?'

'Do not call me that,' he said, and once again, the steeliness of his personality glinted through the urbane exterior. 'I wonder whether it has stopped raining? I thought we might take a little journey on the river tonight. Shall we go and see?'

'A journey on the river?' she queried, looking up at him in surprise as he rose to retrieve her fur wrap.

'Why not? It is, after all, midsummer.'

She stood up as he held her cape open, asking, 'But I must be back at my flat soon, *signor*—'

'There is no one there awaiting you,' he said, his eyes dark on hers. 'No one lying in your bed, no one to welcome you. Come with me instead.'

Kate shuddered slightly as the soft fur brushed her naked arms and neck, then she nestled into the luxurious warmth of it, pulling the sides close about her.

'You are like death, *signor*,' she said half seriously, 'inviting an innocent to come with him, who knows where.'

'You are preoccupied with dying tonight,' he smiled, his splendid face golden, amused. 'Let us go and live a little!'

She strolled beside him along the mews behind the club, the night air cool and delicious on her face.

'Fortunately,' he purred, 'Avis were able to supply me with my usual car.' The cream Lancia lay sleek and glamorous under the watchful eye of an attendant, who opened the door for her. Kate stopped, turning to Carlo.

'Where are you going to take me?' she demanded a little breathlessly.

'To the river,' he replied. 'We have an appointment there.'

'An appointment?'

'Ah, poor Echo,' he mocked, 'is your little heart failing you now? Get in, *cara*. I promise you we are not going far.'

Unwillingly, she slipped in beside him, and settled back rather tensely in the leather seat. The sound of the engine was a tamed snarl that set her heart thudding, but he drove forward smoothly and gently, his hands caressing the wheel carelessly as he urged the car into the dazzling traffic of the wide street. They drove in silence, and Kate gazed out of the window at the glittering lights of London, which shone white and green and red and gold into the interior of the car. She kept her cape wrapped tightly around herself, as though to ward off the threat that Carlo's very presence beside her posed.

He steered the car towards the river which lay dark and wide as night before them, with the lights of the Bankside almost swallowed in its smooth surface. The headlights of the Lancia found a narrow street that led steeply down to the river's bank, and Carlo stopped the car at the head of a flight of steps that descended to the wharf itself. In the silence, Kate could hear the Thames lapping gently at the granite blocks of the wharf. 'Come,' he invited, the white of his teeth gleaming in the shadow.

She shook her head decisively.

'I'm not going a step further until you tell me where exactly you're taking me,' she retorted. 'For all I know, you might be going to drown me in the Thames.'

'What—to claim Leparú all on my own?' he mocked. 'Surely it would be foolish of me to dispose of the only means by which Leparú is mine? That would be burning one's bridges indeed!' He came round to her door, and swung it open. His lithe, perfectly suited figure was silhouetted against the lights on the far side of the bank. 'Come,' he commanded, and she emerged unwillingly from the car. Locking the doors, he led her down the narrow stairs to the echoing water's edge. A boat of some sort was moored there, and as they descended the last steps, a man emerged from the lighted cabin, and saluted.

'Everything in order, sir.'

'Thank you,' murmured Carlo, 'I'll take over from here, Mr Bradshaw.' He turned to Kate with impeccable gallantry, and helped her on to the launch. The man called Bradshaw cast off the mooring-rope while Carlo started the engine throbbing, and then waved goodbye as the launch left the bank and steered out into midstream.

Kate stood in the prow, her heart pounding, and pulled her wrap closer about her. What on earth was happening? Carlo had simply bulldozed her into this madcap adventure, and she had gone along as unresistingly as someone in a dream. She watched the lights receding on the wharf where they had left the Lancia, then glanced upwards. The sky was a deep velvety blue, and the moon shone down brightly, a ghostly galleon drifting among a few last wisps of cloud. The stars were spread above like summer flowers in a meadow, and the gentle night breeze lifted the gold hair at her temples. Suddenly Kate shrugged her mental shoulders. As Beth had said earlier in the day, tonight was a once-in-a-lifetime experience. Why not take it for what it was worth? Don Juan though Carlo might be, she felt strangely certain that he would not take advantage of her here. He was not the sort of man who would use brute power to force his way—it would be infinitely more pleasurable for him to tease, to tempt, to seduce by slow degrees.

In midstream, Carlo cut the engines. As their deep heartbeat faded, he came forward to join her at the brass rail of the prow. The liquid gurgles and ripplings of the water drifted up to them. All was still, but for the distant roar of the city, and the occasional slap of the waves against the hull.

'Who's steering the ship?' Kate asked nervously.

'The rudder is set,' he said calmly, 'and our pilot lights are showing. The current will keep us in mid-channel for miles yet.'

'But where are we going?'

'Wherever the river takes us. Down to Greenwich and beyond, and perhaps out into the sea. Who cares? The tanks are full of fuel, and the night is ours. Come and sit with me, Caterina.'

The front of the boat boasted a long wooden seat, which had been thickly strewn with cushions, like some Eastern divan. He led her away from the rail, and in the mild darkness lay back elegantly against the cushions, looking up at her with a smile.

'Are you cold, *cara*?'

'No,' she answered, sitting demurely beside him, and relaxing a little against the warm luxury of the cushions. The sensation of drifting down the darkened river was delicious, alarming. The bright lights of the City sailed slowly past over them, and she threw her head back as London Bridge passed over them, staring at the mighty arches that towered over head and then were gone. Carlo pulled a wicker basket towards them and opened it.

'Mr Bradshaw has provided us with a flask of coffee,' he said, rummaging in the clinking contents. 'And some brandy, I see. Cold pheasant, potted ham, rolls, peaches —we shall not want. I think a brandy is appropriate now, don't you agree?' He poured a measure into two little silver canisters, passed one over to her, and then lay back in the cushions again.

Kate glanced at him by the light of the City which drifted across to them over the water. He lay with the coiled grace of a leopard, his wide shoulders supported on one elbow, one elegant knee drawn up. His eyes were fixed lazily on the darkness ahead, and she studied his clean, almost aquiline profile, sipping cautiously at the fiery, comforting liquor as she did so. Carlo Castelli was a man who did exactly as he pleased, when he pleased, and with whom he pleased. Behind the tastes of an epicure lay the steely will of a soldier. The night's programme, she knew, had been meticulously planned. For all its flamboyant style, it had been executed with the precision and force of a military engagement. Such cool purpose, such determined efficiency, was something that Kate could admire and respect. It made the flippant mask which Carlo habitually wore easier to understand; yet it also distinguished him as one of the most powerful forces she had ever encountered. As an adversary, Carlo Castelli was terrifying. As a lover? The frankly erotic teasing which was part of his flirtation was difficult enough to deal with. Yet she wondered how she would respond to his real passion. He was the sort of man whose feelings would be staggeringly powerful, whose desire and vitality would be like a volcano erupting. How would she cope with him if ever his inner nature was aroused? At the thought, a quick shudder, half of fear, half voluptuous, ran through her body, and he turned his head quickly to glance at her.

'What thought has touched you, Caterina?'

'Nothing, *signor*—someone stepped over my grave.'

'Your grave—tell me, what is all this talk of dying?' He swung himself fluidly up, and faced her, the moonlight glittering in the deep green depths of his eyes. 'Listen to the peace of the night, Caterina Melville. Nothing will harm you here—I swear it.'

Kate lay back, letting her head roll on a cushion, and gazed up at the stars that drifted overhead, listening to the murmur of the river. What was it saying? What ancient message was it whispering, what secrets rippling?

CHAPTER FOUR

THE launch drifted silently on past the glimmering City. They met no other traffic on the quiet river, and Kate lay entranced, watching the stars that sailed high above in the velvet blue night. When Carlo spoke, his voice was a low purr.

'This will of your Uncle Roger's has put us in a strange position, has it not?'

'How do you mean?' she asked dreamily.

'Had we been an ordinary couple, sitting here in these romantic circumstances, you would by now be in my arms. Nor would we be silent and troubled with mutual distrust.'

'Mutual distrust?' Kate raised herself on one elbow to look at him. 'Do you distrust *me*?' she asked in disbelief.

His chuckle mocked her.

'Do you find that so hard to believe, my dear Kate?'

'But—but—what grounds have I given you to distrust me?' she stammered.

'Surely I have given you no grounds to distrust *me*?' he rejoined.

Kate waved her hand dismissively.

'That's different,' she said. 'You're a strong man. And you're older than I am—I'm the one who should be on guard all the time. No doubt you've seduced dozens of women just as silly as I am.'

'Only dozens?' he enquired gravely. 'You are scarcely flattering in your estimation of my reputation as a seducer of women. Why not hundreds? Even thousands?'

'You may mock me if you wish, *signor*—but you can't tell me that a man with eyes like yours is a stranger to the ways of women!'

'That I do not deny,' he smiled. 'I am not a gelding, Caterina, but a healthy stallion. Yet if you are to hold my eyes against me, surely I can make the same charge against you? You cannot tell me that a woman as beautiful as you has never known the attentions of men?'

'I told you once before, *signor*,' she replied stiffly, 'men have not figured large in my life. I have my art, and I can't permit anything to distract me from it.'

'To call love a distraction,' he said, amused, 'is like calling a typhoon a light breeze.'

'So all lovers say,' retorted Kate. 'But I've never known that feeling.' She glanced at his dark figure beside her. 'Nor do I ever expect to know it.'

'You are impervious, then?'

'Yes,' she said shortly. But her heart had quickened unaccountably, and she knew that in the soft darkness a mocking smile was on that beautiful mouth. The stately buildings of Greenwich were gliding past now, and for a few minutes, she watched them pass by in majestic peace, while Carlo arose to adjust their course in the cabin of the launch.

'Is it late?' she asked when he returned.

'You have nothing to be late for,' he replied, as he settled lithely next to her. She caught the glint of his teeth, and then his hand caressed her face gently. With a gasp, she drew back.

'You forget yourself, Signor Castelli!'

'My intention,' he murmured in his deep, amused voice, 'is to make *you* forget yourself, *cara*. Your memory is

a little obtrusive in these surroundings.' Taking hold of
the soft wings of her cape, he drew her irresistibly to him.
With a yelp of alarm, Kate put her hand on his chest and
pushed. The warm muscles under the silk shirt were as
unyielding as oak, and their touch set her pulse racing.
'Let me go!' she muttered.

'Why are you so afraid?' he asked gently, one strong
hand coming up to touch her lips with extraordinary
gentleness.

'I'm afraid of *you*,' she gasped, 'and it's dark—'

The pressure of his finger stopped her lips.

'The dark is a great liberator,' he murmured, and she
could hear the laughter in his deep voice. 'I have been
watching your mouth all evening, *cara*. And in the end I
decided that its touch would be like warm rose-petals. Yet
I am a scientist as well as a man—and I must test my
theory. Don't you agree?' The question drifted into silence
as his lips brushed hers, lightly, but with an intense
awareness, a deliberate power, that shook her.

'*Signor* —' she whispered.

'There,' he sighed deeply, 'in the end I was wrong. Not
warm rose-petals, but hot silk.'

'Please,' she said urgently, looking into the dark green
glint of his eyes with a drowning helplessness, 'please let
me go, and take me home!'

'The night is yet a maiden,' he smiled, 'like yourself. The
river is long and smooth, and we have many more stars to
see before the dawn comes to call us back. Ah, *tu!* You are
like a schoolgirl in her first illicit orchard, biting into her
first stolen apple!' Again, the fire of his lips touched her,
this time at the corner of her eye. The hand that had been
thrusting at his chest was becoming weak, and Kate found
that her fingers had curled between the buttons of his

shirt. The warm velvet of his skin touched her fingertips as he leaned forward again to kiss the other temple. His breath was warm on her face, and the delicious, faint smell of his after-shave touched her nostrils elusively.

'I trusted you,' she said, as he slipped the cape from her shoulders, 'I trusted you, *signor!*'

'Why do you not trust me still?' he purred, as the fur slithered on to the deck. His hands caressed her bare shoulders for a second, and then were suddenly hard and ruthless as they pulled her body against his.

'You ask me to trust you,' she demanded faintly, 'when you treat me like a slave in some harem?'

'Are you any man's slave?' he asked, his mouth caressing the soft skin at the side of her neck. 'I think not, Caterina. You are—' his teeth brushed her skin for an instant, making her shudder, '—a being of snow and ice, impervious to the flames of passion. Am I not correct?'

Kate arched her neck to the delicious torment of his kisses at her throat, her body straining to comply with his desire. Then her mind reasserted itself, and she ran her fingers desperately into his thick hair, clenching hard, and drew herself away.

'For the love of God, *signor,* let me be!' Yet even as she met his dark gaze, her fingers relaxed involuntarily, and the act of violence changed imperceptibly into a sensual caress, as her fingers explored the crisp, warm hair at the back of his head.

'*Tigressa!*' he murmured, the laughter gurgling in his throat.

'*Diavolo!*' she retorted, flinging herself away from him, tears of shame and anger stinging her eyes. He followed her with a panther's quickness, and as she collapsed back against the cushions in the prow of the launch, he was at her side, an elbow either side of her arms, gazing down into her face.

'Is the apple not sweet enough, my little schoolgirl?' he asked mockingly. 'Are you afraid the farmer will suddenly appear and chase you away, with your pigtails flying?'

'I—' Once again, his mouth brushed hers, harder now, more demandingly. 'I am no schoolgirl, *signor*,' she said breathlessly. 'Why do you insist on mocking me like this?'

'You are full of courage, at least,' he said softly. 'Do you want me to stop?'

'Of course I do,' she snapped, lying back helplessly beneath his dark gaze.

'Then you feel no passion at all?'

'None,' she said shakily, feeling the blood pounding at her throat as she spoke the word. 'I am, as you say, *signor*, a being of ice.'

'Really?' His lips touched hers with the delicacy of a butterfly's wing, and the very lightness of the caress made her heart leap as no roughness could ever do.

'Really,' she answered, but her voice was almost a whisper. Then his mouth claimed hers with supreme authority, and a shuddering weakness washed over her. She made up her mind desperately to remain completely still, willing her lips to stay cool, not to respond to his kiss. She concentrated on the whisper and sigh of the water against the boat's side as his lips pressed hers, warm and firm, at each corner of her mouth, then full on the lips. She clenched her teeth, squeezing her eyes shut, and balling her fists helplessly at her sides. His laughter was as infinitely amused as a devil's in her ear.

'Poor little hedgehog! Is it worth resisting? Even to escape the possession of a little piece of paradise?'

Kate lay stubborn and silent, her teeth tightly clenched,

willing him to release her. But he did not; and when his teeth took her lower lip with sudden, wickedly mischievous force, and bit. She could not suppress a gasp, and her eyes flew open.

'You're cruel!'

'All's fair, *cara*, in this kind of warfare.' Then his lips were pressed to hers again, meeting them with shameless delight, tasting the secrets within. Kate struggled madly, yet her own trembling movements were ambiguous. The arms that wrestled free of his did so only in order to creep around his neck; the hands that tensed themselves to scratch ended up caressing his thick hair. With the irresistible playfulness of a huge cat, he rolled on to his back, pulling her on top of him. Panting, she gazed down at his face, seeing the moon reflected brilliantly in each deep green eye.

'Let me go!' she snapped.

'So,' he smiled lazily, contentedly, 'a little fire runs in your veins after all!'

'Let me go,' she demanded, thanking heaven for the darkness which concealed her crimson face, 'you're hurting me, *signor!*'

'My name is Carlo,' he purred. 'Is it not time that you used my first name, *cara?*'

'I don't know you well enough,' she snapped angrily. 'Let me go!'

His silent laughter shook her. 'Are we not on sufficiently intimate terms yet?'

Suddenly she became aware of her position on top of him. Through the fine silk of her dress, she could feel the hard strength of his body, and one of her thighs had slipped between his. With a little pant of dismay, she tried to pull loose, but his arms were immovable around her waist, and she thrust at his iron chest in vain. 'I want to be free!' she demanded hotly.

He shook his head at her imperturbably.

'Not until you ask me by my name,' he grinned.

'Let me go—Carlo,' she gritted.

'Once more—and this time politely, or we shall stay here all night.'

'Let me go, Carlo—*please!*'

He released her, and she rolled away, brushing the soft hair that had fallen around her face into some semblance of order. Carlo was on his feet in one swift movement, checking their distance from the bank. 'We're still holding course, he said calmly. 'Come and see.'

Kate looked at his outstretched hand suspiciously, and then took it. With smooth power, he pulled her to her feet, and led her to the bow-rail. They had left London behind them already, and the Thames was flowing through dark countryside now. Kate could see fields and a few farms stretching away to the west, and to the east, a long line of trees. Was it her imagination, or had the darkness lightened slightly?

As if reading her thoughts, Carlo murmured, 'It will be dawn soon.' A little breeze made her shiver slightly, and he picked up her wrap and laid it over her shoulders. She pulled the fur gratefully about her, and as the launch rounded a wide bend in the river, the long streak of ruby light in the east came into view.

Carlo went back into the wheelhouse and began to steer the launch towards the bank.

'We'll watch the sun come up from here,' he called, 'and have a little breakfast. I'm ravenous—and you?'

'I couldn't eat a thing,' she said shortly. The long shape of the launch drifted smoothly into the grassy slope of the bank. Kate could see flowers blooming among the lush grass, and the grey light of early dawn silvered the venerable trunks of the ancient oaks. As the launch slowed in the eddying water, Carlo leaped quickly on to the shore and moored the boat by its rope to one of the trees. The launch tugged with gentle impatience at its mooring for an instant, and then relapsed into obedient stillness. Carlo stepped back on to the deck, holding a wild cyclamen in his hand. It was still wet and cool with dew as he slipped it into her golden hair, and smiled into her eyes.

'Good morning, *cara*.' Unwilling to forgive him, she looked away. It was a beautiful spot indeed. The water eddied with a delicious chuckle around the stern of the launch, and the willow-trees that overhung them sighed gently in the early morning breezes. Across the river, which had begun to gleam like burnished silver, the flat hills and rich farmlands stretched away to the first glow of the coming sunrise. In the peaceful stillness, a moorhen drifted past, followed by her five chicks, no more than balls of dark fluff on the surface of the water. A lark, invisibly high in the steel-blue heaven, had begun to sing, and somewhere, miles away, a rooster crowed.

'Do you like the place?' he asked.

'It's lovely,' she admitted unwillingly. He took her arm with a smile, and led her back to the cushions. By the gathering light, she could see that his dress was as immaculate as it had been when she had first met him at the St James'—it seemed like years ago. The wicked beauty of his face was heart-stopping, and the pre-dawn light had toned the midnight green of his eyes into their usual smoky emerald luminence.

'Have some pheasant, Caterina—you must be hungry, no matter what you say. And some of this cold salad, too.

Do you like pickles?' He passed the laden plate to her with a grin, and opened the flask of coffee. Its sweet fragrance perfumed the morning air, and the growling in Kate's stomach redoubled. Deciding to let dignity wait on necessity this time, she tucked into her meal with the relish of a schoolgirl, and he watched her with ironic amusement for a few seconds, before turning to his own coffee.

The brilliant carmine rim of the sun edged over the grey horizon, filling the sky with a red-gold glory. The few clouds in the sky became purple silk, shot with yellow and crimson, and the bright stain seeped upwards into the heavens. Kate watched, spellbound, as the majesty of the sun emerged from night, shedding its dazzling radiance into the earth's atmosphere. Soon it was too dazzling to look at, and the blessed warmth of its beams caressed her face and arms. She turned to Carlo, all the resentment and struggling of the night melting away in the presence of this vast beauty, and smiled.

'Thank you for bringing me here, Carlo. It's wonderful!'

The irony in his glance faded abruptly, and a smile of real pleasure curved his lips. He inclined his head gently in acknowledgment, and Kate stared at him intently as he turned back to look up the long, glittering scimitar of the river. His natural presence was astounding—he had a dignity, an authority, that was undeniable. She knew that only the darkness had saved her from melting into his arms during the brief summer night—for had there been light enough to see that stern, golden face with its leopard's eyes, she knew she would have been unable to resist.

Now the sun was a mass of golden flame, free of the earth's grasp, and the sky had become a tender, milky blue. It was going to be a lovely day. Kate finished the delicious cold pheasant, and stood up to take Carlo's plate. He grinned.

'I think I saw some wild strawberries on the bank,' he said. 'We have no cream, I'm afraid, but perhaps they will be ripe enough to eat.' He stepped ashore, while Kate washed the plates in the galley, and packed them back into the wicker basket. She had finished brushing her flaxen hair in the mirror by the time Carlo had come aboard again, his cupped hands holding a little heap of the tiny crimson strawberries.

'*Fraises des bois,*' he smiled. 'When I was a child, I used to gather these in the fields outside Agrigentum, and bring them home to my grandmother. Try one.'

The tiny wild fruits were icy cold, and covered with dew; but they were sweet and perfumed, and they left a fragrance on the tongue that was as charming as youth. They ate them all, sharing a moment of intimacy, as the sun climbed up into the sky. A distant tractor began to chug somewhere, and the birds had begun to fill the clean air.

'I think we'd better get some rest, little hedgehog,' he said gently. 'The day is beginning already, and you and I must meet again this afternoon.'

'This afternoon? Oh no!' Kate shook her head vigorously. 'When I get back to London, Signor Castelli, I'm going to run as far and as fast as I can!'

'What for?'

'To escape you, of course.'

'You cannot escape this time,' he grinned. 'For we must get down to business in the end. Besides, I have already arranged the meeting.'

'With whom?'

'With your second cousin, Vera de Cruz. We are all meeting for tea at Claridges this afternoon at four.'

'I'm not coming,' she said briskly. But Carlo shook his head with authority, his eyes meeting hers with irresistible command.

'You *must* come,' he told her. 'We must all discuss Roger's mad will.'

She opened her mouth to argue, then closed it again, and relapsed into silence.

Carlo unhitched the launch from its mooring, and stepped into the wheelhouse. The sun was high by now, and the summer's day was growing warm. The engine of the boat began to throb like a great heart in the water, and he glanced at her through the Perspex of the cabin.

'Are you ready?' he called. She nodded. The engines rumbled with sudden power, and the launch curved out into the channel, cutting a silver swathe in the water. The bow-wave rippled out among the nodding reeds, and Kate cast a last farewell glance at the spot, before the turn was complete and they were steaming up the Thames to London.

Vera poised a crumpet delicately between finger and thumb, and fluttered her thick eyelashes at Carlo.

'Really?' she drawled. 'How utterly fascinating!' She had made herself as beautiful as she knew how for this occasion, and Kate was forced to acknowledge that she looked ravishing. The dark red suit was perhaps a little formal for an afternoon engagement, but its deep tone set off Vera's rather pale skin well. The wings of blue eye-shadow over each dark eye were dramatic, and her ruby lipstick completed a sultry, almost orchid-like ensemble. She was elegant, thought Kate, sophisticated.

While she herself, Kate knew, was looking slightly tired, and the simple cream dress she wore was no match for Vera's flame-like brilliance. She had slept the whole morning away after the Lancia had dropped her at Wimbledon, and she was still a little sleepy at four o'clock, despite the pleasures of tea at Claridges. Whereas Carlo was as splendid as ever in a pale grey suit that had been cut by a supreme artist. The strength and vitality in the tawny eyes was undiminished, and with his jet-black hair and his gold-tinted skin, he looked as out of place drinking tea at Claridges as a tiger smiling among sheep.

He leaned back in his chair, crossing his legs, and surveyed Vera with serious eyes.

'But what of yourself?' he asked. 'Kate tells me that you were born in Madrid.'

'Yes,' said Vera, brushing crumbs off her fingertips with an elegant gesture. 'My father was an officer in the Royal Bodyguard at the Palace there. He met my mother at a polo match when the Spanish team toured Britain one year. They fell in love and—well, here I am.' She smiled brightly.

'How romantic,' smiled Carlo. 'I have played some polo myself in my time. As a matter of fact, I believe my father once went with a team to play in Spain.'

'Really?' gushed Vera. 'I wonder whether our fathers ever met?'

'It's not impossible,' he said gravely. 'Now let me see—what year would that have been . . .'

Kate sighed inwardly, and sipped from her tea-cup. Vera's behaviour had been utterly predictable. When she had arrived, Carlo and Vera had already been deep in conversation, and neither had spoken more than a sentence to her since she had sat down. Nor was it the sort of

conversation which Kate felt equipped to join. Vera had
led a somewhat spoiled life, and her knowledge of the way
life was lived at the top enabled her to regale Carlo with
the sort of name-dropping conversation which Kate pre-
sumed was *de rigueur* among the jet-set. Carlo and Vera
had apparently skied in the same resorts, safaried in the
same game reserves, met the same millionaires and film
stars. They had both watched the total eclipse of the sun
from Reykjavik. And now, it seemed, both had descended
from polo-playing military fathers. And from the suppres-
sed excitement on Vera's pale, beautiful face, Kate knew
that her cousin had succumbed utterly to Carlo's virile
charm.

'Oh yes,' she was saying eagerly, 'we played polo at
school, you know—it was frightfully amusing, of course,
and strictly forbidden. You should have seen all the
schoolgirl riders! Though I was one of the better ones, I
must admit.'

'And you, Kate?' he asked, turning to her.

She coughed a little into her tea.

'Well,' she said, 'we played netball at the Girls' High.
And—er—tennis, and—'

'As a matter of fact,' interrupted Vera smoothly, 'last
summer I happened to meet Sir Gordon Arnold at Can-
nes—do you know Sir Gordon? He helped to train the
Bolivian team. Well, he told me . . .'

Kate munched at a cream scone glumly, and stared
around the delightfully-furnished room, with its calm,
thirties atmosphere. A faint depression had settled over
her. The fantastic glamour of the night before seemed to
have faded like a dream. She watched Carlo's beautiful,
masculine face as he listened intently to Vera's gush, and
wondered whether he could possibly be really interested.

And whether she should acknowledge the niggling jealousy that had started as soon as she saw Carlo and Vera in conversation, and that was now turning the cream scones to ashes in her mouth. A name she thought she recognised drifted into the conversation.

'Oh,' she said suddenly, 'Charles Armstrong?' Carlo and Vera turned to her, Carlo with interest, Vera with ill-disguised impatience. 'Charles Armstrong the painter?' she asked. 'I know him! I met him at Bangor one—'

'I was referring to Charles Armstrong the racehorse owner,' cut in Vera acidly.

'Oh,' said Kate in a different tone. 'Oh—well, I don't know *him*. But Charles Armstrong the painter—'

'As I was saying, my dear Carlo,' continued Vera, laying a slender, red-nailed hand on Carlo's elegantly-suited arm, 'the ballet had been *frightfully* bad that year and . . .'

Kate snapped at the rest of the cream scone as though it was a mouse and she a hungry, ill-tempered cat. Carlo's attention was once more intent on Vera. Why did he not even glance at her? she wondered angrily. He could at least give her a little smile to show that he was as bored by Vera's flow of speech as she was. After all, they had been almost—well, almost close in the radiant dawn. She studied Vera's smooth face resentfully. Surely Carlo wasn't being taken in by Vera de Cruz's sophisticated veneer? Why, Vera was practically a middle-aged woman! With horrible clarity, her own words to Beth Hussey about Vera came back to her mind—'she's only thirty, and she's very good-looking . . .' Kate's heart sank into her grey court shoes. Could Carlo really—? The thought was too horrible to contemplate. Carlo might be a Don Juan, but at the thought that he might seriously be fascinated by Vera, her blood unaccountably boiled. A sudden desire to wipe the smug, pseudo-sultry smile from Vera's pretty face got the better of Kate. She put down her tea-cup and leaned forward.

'Carlo,' she said, as huskily as her clear soprano voice would allow, 'I haven't had the chance to thank you for a wonderful evening last night. It was so beautiful, and so romantic.' The frozen expression that settled on Vera's features made her heart rise. 'I can't remember when I've enjoyed myself so much,' she added, picking up her tea-cup in triumph.

Vera turned icily to Carlo, raising her devastating eyebrow for an explanation. Carlo's face did not change.

'I took Kate to dinner last night,' he said. *Kate*, not Caterina! 'I thought it would do her good to get out of her flat and see a little life. I telephoned your hotel,' he said, inclining his head to Vera, 'but you were unfortunately out.'

'Was I?' smiled Vera contentedly. 'I may have gone down to the West End for a little late-night shopping.'

'Ah. Well, in the event, I took Kate back to my club for a bite of dinner. Though she seemed to find it all rather overwhelming at the time.'

Vera sniggered, glancing maliciously at Kate, and then, satisfied with what Carlo had said, launched herself back into her story. Kate felt as though a bucket of iced water had suddenly been hurled into her face. She sat numb, rigid. A bite of dinner? Rather overwhelmed? Tears of furious mortification started to her eyes, and she felt the blood rushing to her face. She had never been so coolly, effectively snubbed in her life. Vera and Carlo were so engrossed in one another's talk that the scarlet in Kate's cheeks had time to seep away, leaving her face a pearly white. Mechnically, she set down her tea-cup, feeling her heart thudding with leaden blows against her ribs. She was not going to forgive Carlo for snubbing her like this! Just as she was about to excuse herself with a few icy words, and walk out of the hotel, he clapped his hands softly and glanced at both women.

'That is enough gossip for the time being,' he said firmly. 'We shall have to resume this most fascinating conversation later.' Vera bridled, drooping her long lashes at Carlo. 'Let us talk business for a few seconds. Now, I presume by now you have all opened the packages which Roger Courtney left you?' They nodded. 'I am going to be quite frank, and say that mine contained a letter of some personal interest, and a cheque for five thousand pounds.'

'So did mine,' admitted Vera. Kate nodded silently.

'Very well,' Carlo continued. 'Roger has put the three of us in a rather impossible position with this extraordinary will of his.' His magnificent eyes flicked from Vera to Kate. 'Quite what was in his mind, I am at a loss to say. Roger was an almost pathological joker, as you both know. Although I must admit that this is the first time I have failed to be amused by one of his little pranks. This one strikes me as being in rather questionable taste.'

'Hear, hear,' murmured Vera.

'But *de mortuis nil nisi bonum*, as my Latin master would have said. We must leave Roger's secret buried with Roger. I wish him no ill—may he rest in peace. But for us, the living, one crucial question remains. The island of Leparú.'

Vera's eyes glittered brightly, and Kate could tell that her breathing had quickened. As for herself, the name struck on her ears with a leaden, almost sinister sound.

'I wish I'd never heard of Leparú,' she sighed.

Carlo turned to her, his golden face serious.

'But you have heard of it, my dear Kate. And we must now make a few decisions about the next few weeks. As I said before, I'm going to put all my cards on the table. Leparú is a most beautiful place. Neither of you have seen it. I have had the advantage of having visited the island many, many times during Roger's lifetime, and I can assure you that it is a precious, wonderful place. It is also worth a great deal of money. Mr Potter of Potter, Bush and Linford estimates it to be worth one quarter of a million pounds sterling. It may sell for considerably less than that, of course—but it is certainly an expensive piece of property.'

There was a hush, broken only by the chatter of some elderly ladies at a distant table. Vera's eyes met Kate's for a second, then slid away. In that moment, Kate knew that Vera would do anything in her power to seize Carlo, and claim the island for herself. The thought chilled Kate unpleasantly.

'As for myself, I may as well admit to you both that I am not a poor man,' continued Carlo. 'I have taken this trip to London with the specific purpose of seeing you two ladies—the financial aspect of the whole affair does not interest me at all.'

'My dear Carlo, you amaze me,' drawled Vera, her expert eyebrow challenging his statement coolly.

Carlo's smile was brief.

'I am the sole stockholder of a very large corporation, my dear ladies, which manufactures micro-circuitry for a vast range of purposes. I have very large holdings in several other factories which produce computers and calculating equipment. My sphere of interest in Europe is equivalent to IBM or Burroughs in the United States.' He sipped calmly from his tea-cup, and surveyed them both. 'I have been lucky enough to ride to fortune on the electronics boom of the past ten years. My computers are in every city in every country in Europe, and beyond. The whole operation, which is called Data-Castelli, is worth several million pounds. I'm not quite sure how many,' he smiled. 'Perhaps twenty-five or thirty million. A lot of money.'

The hush was even more intense now. Kate's heart was thudding. Thirty million pounds? Had she really imagined that Carlo Castelli could have had the faintest interest in her? And her little games with him last night— what madness it had been to presume that her schoolgirl antics could have the slightest interest for this man! She glanced at Vera's white, tense face. Unless Carlo was lying—

'You may check this information,' he said gently, 'at any newspaper office.' His eyes met hers. It was as though he had read her mind. It was Vera who found her tongue first.

'You're not pulling my leg, Carlo Castelli?'

'I assure you I am not,' he said, unoffended. 'It sounds a vast amount of money, I agree. But of course, ninety per cent of it is locked tightly away in the various companies I operate. Should I wish to play around, alas,' he smiled, 'I would have only a few paltry hundred thousands. To raise more I should have to sell stock.'

'I see,' said Vera softly. Her eyes were shining. 'Then the island of Leparú is of no more consequence to you than the cream scone you've just eaten?'

'That would be an exaggeration,' he said, amused. 'I merely wished to point out that among the three of us,

Leparú has a quite different impact. It means something different to each of the three of us.'

'I'll say,' agreed Vera somewhat breathlessly. Kate stared at Carlo, spellbound.

'I presume,' he asked, 'that neither of you is in the same tax bracket as I am?' Somehow the question was neither mocking nor ridiculous, and the two women shook their heads solemnly.

'Well,' said Carlo Castelli, 'it seems to me that of the three of us, I deserve Leparú the least. Roger Courtney was, after all, your relation, and not mine. And quite frankly, I would prefer the two of you to have the pleasure—or the value—of Leparú between you. Yet it would seem a shame to sell the island without enjoying the wonderful beauty of it. And luckily, Roger has left provision for just this situation in his will. I have a proposition.'

'Well,' said Vera eagerly, 'let's hear it, brother!'

'Are you interested, Kate?' he asked, meeting her eyes directly.

'Yes,' she nodded, finding her voice at last. 'Please tell us what you think.'

'Then what I propose is this. Let us go to Leparú—the three of us. It is now high summer, and the island will be coming into its best time. I need a long holiday I have been working far too hard to make my millions lately. And Roger has left each of you enough money to cover the journey there and back, with a generous spending allowance into the bargain. I know that both of you can afford to take a break at this time. So, we go. We enjoy Leparú for as long as the summer lasts—three months of paradise. Then, in the autumn, we will spin a coin. Whichever of you two wins—or loses,' he smiled, 'I will marry. Then we will divorce a week later, sell the island, and divide the proceeds between the two of you. I will want nothing. We will part, on the best of terms, and never see each other's faces again.' He picked up his tea-cup again, and his golden-green eyes met Kate's with power and beauty. 'Now tell me—what do you think of that?'

CHAPTER FIVE

KATE emerged from her bedroom the next morning, blinking in the morning sunlight, and made her way to the kitchen for a reviving cup of coffee. She caught sight of the wild cyclamen that Carlo had picked for her on the banks of the Thames. She had taken the flower from her hair on her return, and had placed it in a vase, and its shell-pink petals were still moist and fresh. She stroked the sensuous flower absently while the kettle boiled, and then took her coffee through into the living-room, and curled up on the sofa to think things over.

Somehow it had all been too much to take in the night before—the news of Carlo's wealth and power, his proposition about Leparú. She had needed a good night's sleep to get her thoughts in order.

Her attitude towards Carlo Castelli had suffered some drastic changes since the little tea-party at Claridges Hotel the afternoon before. The revelation that he was a supremely successful and powerful man had not come as a total surprise. She recalled little remarks he had dropped earlier—'I am a man of the present . . . I am a scientist . . .' No, it was not the fact of Carlo's wealth that had taken her aback. It was the whole change in his manner. She had seen a completely new side of Carlo over the tea-table—a ruthless, urbane businessman, who could talk polo and skiing and privilege with complete assurance; who could snub her so wickedly in front of Vera de

Cruz; and who could be hard-headed enough to make the proposal he had made concerning the island.

It was that, in the end, which had hurt Kate—the casualness with which he had discussed marriage and divorce, simply as ways to make money. Despite her platonic relations with the men in her life, Kate cherished old-fashioned views about the sanctity of marriage; and to hear Carlo proposing so casually to marry either of them, simply to secure Leparú, had shocked her deeply. She thought back to the dreamlike beauty of the trip down the river, the magnificent sunrise, the emerald light in Carlo's eyes. Could the same man have been responsible for both ideas? The one so deliciously romantic, the other so sordidly practical?

'Be honest with yourself, Kate,' she muttered. 'You didn't care much for his romantic side either, did you?' No, it was true, she had spent most of the night fighting him, struggling with him. Neither aspect of Carlo's nature had really pleased her—she had been frankly terrified of his desire, infuriated by his teasing, and now she was offended by his businesslike pragmatism.

'He's simply an unlikeable man,' she decided firmly. A powerful man, yes, and someone who had an almost electric effect on people around him—but not a man to like or trust.

The telephone interrupted her reverie, and she got up to answer it. It was Beth Hussey.

'What's been going on?' she asked excitedly. 'I've been ringing you since yesterday morning. Have you decided to elope, or what?'

Despite herself, Kate smiled.

'No,' she said, 'I'm still here, Beth.'

'Well, did you go to the St James' with him?'

'What? Oh—that. Yes, I went along in the end.'

'And what happened? Did he seduce you?'

'No,' Kate grinned.

'Did you seduce *him*, then?'

'It's a very long story, Beth. Let's meet for lunch, and I'll tell you all about it.'

'Great! Come round to my place—I've got some couscous and lamb stew that you'll simply love.'

'I'm on a diet,' said Kate hastily. 'Let's just have a snack somewhere—say that place off Leicester Square that we liked so much. I'll see you there about one. Okay?'

'I can't wait,' said Beth. 'See you then.'

Kate put down the receiver, and went into her bedroom to dress.

She had been painting for an hour when the doorbell rang. When she opened the door, she was surprised to see Mark Watson standing on her doorstep, holding a large parcel. Mark, a pleasant, moustachioed young man, had taken her to dinner on several occasions, and she had enjoyed his company. He was also secretary of the Wild Flower Preservation Trust, and Kate suspected that he was there in his business capacity that morning. She was not mistaken.

'Hi, Kate,' he said, kissing her on the cheek, 'I'm glad I've caught you in this morning. Can I come in?'

'Hello, Mark—sure, come in.'

He put the parcel carefully on the table and turned to her.

'I wonder if you could do us a big favour, Kate. One of our members happens to have found some extremely rare orchids recently, and we'd like a painting of them for the front cover of this year's bulletin. Would you be able to oblige, do you think?'

'I suppose so,' she smiled. 'Get the precious things out, while I make a pot of tea.'

By the time she had returned with a tray, Mark had reverently laid the three plants on a sheet of newspaper. Each had had its roots carefully bound up in wet peat.

'I'm surprised your friend was allowed to gather them,' said Kate, coming over to examine the strange flowers.

'Oh, they'll have to be replaced,' he replied. 'As soon as you've done with them, we'll take them back and re-plant them in exactly the same site.'

'I see,' said Kate, passing him the biscuits. 'They're odd-looking things, aren't they? But very beautiful.'

'The yellow and purple one is Lady's Slipper,' he told her. 'It's very rare indeed. It's the first one I've ever seen. The other two are also very uncommon. The velvety pink one is called *fuciflora*—the Late Spider Orchid, and that one is called the Man Orchid.'

'That's a strange name,' she said, examining the plant more closely. Then she gave a little cry of surprise. 'Why, it's covered with little men!'

'Yes,' he smiled. 'It was found near the Spider Orchid.'

Kate looked at the little plant in wonder. The dangling pink petals all over the long stem were shaped exactly like tiny human figures. It was an uncannily weird and beautiful plant. 'I've never seen anything like it,' she said. 'I'm going to enjoy painting that.'

'Those two came from Devon,' Mark told her, drinking his tea. 'The Lady's Slipper came from Durham. They'll have to be put back at the dead of night, in great secrecy. They're quite precious, and people will go to great lengths to steal a specimen.'

'Really?'

'Oh yes. It can be quite a cut-throat business—the

same as rare birds' eggs. Unscrupulous collectors would spirit those plants away if they found them, and England would have three fewer rare plants. You'll have to keep the whole thing quiet,' he grinned, 'or someone will burgle your flat. When do you think you'll be finished?'

She thought a bit. 'To-morrow afternoon, I should think.'

'Terrific. Just put the roots in a basin of water, and they'll be fine. Listen, Kate—how about coming out with me to-night? There's a party at Sean Carney's place. We could maybe have a Chinese dinner first?'

Kate looked at Mark's open, youthful face, and could not help comparing him mentally to Carlo's mature poise and power. The thought of another of Mark's friends' parties depressed her suddenly, and she shook her head regretfully. 'I'm sorry, Mark, but I—er—have to work late to-night, especially if I'm to get these orchids finished.'

'Ah well,' said Mark, obviously disappointed. 'You work a lot too hard, Kate. You should take a holiday some time.'

'It's funny you should say that,' she said wryly. 'Some-one's just offered to let me use a holiday home in Sicily.'

'Sicily? That sounds wonderful! You're not going to turn down an offer like that?'

'I'm afraid I am,' she said. 'I'm a working girl, and I have to earn my living. Besides, I'm already overloaded with commissions—I can't just walk out on them all.'

Mark looked at her strangely as he prepared to leave.

'Can I ask a personal question, Kate? You don't ever feel that life is passing you by, do you?'

And Beth said much the same thing, over their pizza.

'But you *must* go, Kate! This chance won't come again.'

'I don't like the idea at all, Beth. It's so—so inhuman, to talk about marriage as though it were some sort of industrial contract.'

'Well, you don't have to take any part in that, Kate. After all, your uncle Roger has left you five thousand quid—it's more or less your duty to go and visit the old boy's island.'

'I don't know . . .' Kate stirred her ravioli into patterns absently. 'The thought of being cooped up on a desert island with Vera and Carlo is enough to put anyone off. She'll be all over him, anyway—it'll be nauseating to watch her.'

Beth looked at her friend with alert eyes, her silver ear-bobs swinging.

'You haven't let this Carlo get under your skin, have you?'

'Why do you say that?'

'You sound a bit jealous of Vera, that's all.'

'Well, she *is* sickening,' said Kate defensively. 'And Carlo Castelli means nothing to me.'

'Are you quite sure of that?' asked Beth thoughtfully.

'Quite sure. And I'm convinced I mean even less to *him*.'

'Even though he must have spent a couple of hundred pounds laying on that royal entertainment for you the other night?' Beth shook her head doubtfully, and gulped at her beer.

'Come on, Beth—you don't imagine a man worth millions of pounds, with a face and figure like Carlo's could possibly be interested in a little nobody from Wimbledon?'

'I've told you before,' smiled Beth, 'you're a very

beautiful girl, Kate. It wouldn't surprise me at all to learn
that Carlo was interested in you.'

'As a night's amusement, maybe. Seriously—never.'

'Well, as long as you're certain. Shall we try the ice-
cream, or is your diet too strict?'

Over the ice-cream, Kate asked Beth, 'What makes you
think I should go to Leparú?'

'To see it, for one thing. An artist should be open to
experience. That's what I believe. It may do your art a
great deal of good to see Leparú—cobalt skies and golden
beaches, etcetera.'

'You sound just like Carlo,' Kate said drily.

'Well, it's true. Have you ever been to the Mediterranean?'

'I went on a package tour to France and Italy two years
ago,' said Kate.

Beth shook her head.

'That's not what I meant. To understand a place, you
have to *live* in it, not just pass through it. This island
sounds like heaven on earth. Kate, just think of the
pictures you could paint there! It might give you a whole
new slant on your painting technique. After all, the light's
different there— everything's different. Life's too short for
caution, old chum—if you miss this chance, you'll suddenly find yourself a lonely old thing in a garret with a
smelly cat, with not a single memory to console you.'

Kate smiled. 'I intend to age with dignity,' she said. 'I
shall be an interesting and very aristocratic Miss Melville
with a Persian grey—not a lonely old thing with a smelly
cat.'

'And as for Vera and Carlo—well, you can just leave
them to it. If Vera thinks she can snare him, then good
luck to her. You can spend all day on the beach alone,

basking in the sun, or painting, or chatting up the local mermen, or something.'

'It sounds pleasant,' Kate admitted. 'But I listened to you last time, and look where it got me.'

'Yeah—it got you the most romantic evening of your life! So don't be ungrateful!'

'D'you want coffee? Neither do I. Let's go and sit in Leicester Square and watch the pigeons.'

They paid for their meal, and strolled down to the little green in the middle of the square. The statue of Shakespeare gazed serenely over their heads as they found a bench and sat down.

'Where's Carlo to-day?' asked Beth.

Kate shrugged. 'Buying up Hampshire or something. I don't really care. We're supposed to give him our answers to-night.'

'You're really down on him, aren't you?'

'I'm just totally different from him, Beth. He's an unscrupulous business man and I'm—'

'You're a little saint, aren't you?' said Beth mockingly. 'It hasn't occurred to you that Signor Castelli is being uncommonly generous about this whole show, has it?'

'What do you mean?'

'Well, he's offered to marry either you or Vera—which is pretty heroic, when you come to think of it—and he doesn't want a penny for his services, either. He's an important man, Kate, for heaven's sake! Why should he bother with two miserable Englishwomen and a desert island? Quite frankly, if *I* were him, I'd say to the devil with all of you, and get back to making my fortune.'

'I didn't see it quite like that,' mused Kate. She looked up at the huge cinema poster across the street. The title of the film, in letters six feet high, was SWEET POISON. Somehow the title seemed ominous to her.

'You can't be that busy that you couldn't take a break for six weeks,' prodded Beth.

'I was telling Mark Watson how busy I was only this morning,' sighed Kate. 'But now I'm not so sure. All your talk of golden sands has set me dreaming, I must confess.' As if to reinforce her words, there was a rumble of thunder, and a sudden patter of rain sent the pigeons whirring into the air.

'Typical English summer weather,' commented Beth.

'It'll probably rain for weeks. And Sicily is one of the warmest places in Europe, so I've heard.'

'I wonder . . .'

'Gosh, if I had your chances, Kate! You don't know when you're well off. And if it turns out miserable, you can always come straight home again. You've got all that money, don't forget.'

'You make it sound so easy,' said Kate, watching the pigeons settling in the eaves of the Odeon.

'Why are you so anxious about it?' asked Beth, puzzled. 'You're not afraid of Carlo, are you?'

Kate pulled a wry face. 'You haven't seen him—I have. I think I'd rather closet myself with a grown lion than with Carlo Castelli!'

'Then you're not going to go?' asked Beth, plainly disappointed.

Kate sighed.

'I don't think I am, no.'

'Not going?' Vera's voice was shrill, and Kate removed the telephone from her ear slightly. 'But what are you talking about, girl—you *can't* not go!'

'I just don't have the time, Vera, and—'

'Don't talk nonsense, Katherine! You have plenty of time. Roger left you five thousand pounds, didn't he?'

'Yes, he did. But—'

'Then stop all this childish argument, Katherine. You're coming to Leparú, and that's an end of it.'

'I don't understand why you're so indignant about it,' rejoined Kate, beginning to grow angry. 'My life is my own, and if I don't want to go, I won't.'

'I don't know how you can be so selfish,' shrilled Vera, and Kate was astonished to hear the tears in her voice. 'It's *very* unkind of you! Why can't you think of someone else for a change?'

'Vera, for goodness' sake! I thought you were going to be pleased that I wasn't coming.'

'Why should I be pleased?' crackled the telephone furiously.

Kate looked blankly at the afternoon sunlight on the windowsill.

'But I thought you'd want to have Carlo all to yourself on Leparú, Vera. Surely you don't want me along?'

'You don't understand, you idiot,' squeaked Vera. 'Carlo won't come to Leparú unless you're there. He won't go if it's just going to be me!'

'How do you know that?' asked Kate curiously.

There was a pregnant pause.

'I—er—I asked him,' said Vera at length.

'What did you ask him?'

'After you left last night—I asked him whether he wouldn't like to come to the island with me alone. Without you, that is.' Kate said nothing, feeling curiously angry, and Vera's voice became defensive, embarrassed. 'Well, all's fair and all that, Katherine. You'd have done the same thing if you'd had the brains to think of it.'

'Would I?' said Kate coldly.

'Well, you made it plain enough that you're not interested in Carlo, sweetie,' said Vera righteously. 'And, speaking quite frankly, you *are* a little young for him, aren't you?'

'If you say so, Vera,' said Kate frigidly, trying not to let her anger show. 'It's not really very relevant.'

'Exactly,' crackled Vera with relief. 'The point is whether you're coming to Leparú or not. Because if you don't come, you'll be doing *me* out of *my* inheritance as well!'

'I wouldn't want to do that,' said Kate drily.

'You ought to have lot more consideration for others, Katherine. You were always selfish, even as a child. I remember my mother saying once—'

'I've just changed my mind,' said Kate quietly.

'What's that?'

'I'm going to come after all, Vera.'

'Well, I should think so,' said Vera with satisfaction. 'And I'm glad to hear you admit once and for all that Carlo Castelli is out of your class.'

'Is he?'

'Of course he is, child! You don't dream that he's interested in you, do you? Now, I want your solemn promise that you're not going to get under our feet in Leparú. I shall want Signor Castelli all to myself on this holiday, and I shall expect *you* to give us a wide berth. You do understand what I'm saying, Katherine?'

'Oh, I understand all right,' said Kate through clenched teeth.

'I'm glad to hear it. And I trust you're not going to make yourself obtrusive?'

For a few seconds, Kate's mind boggled with so many sarcastic replies that she was speechless.

'You'll have to excuse me, I'm afraid,' she said at last, looking at the sunlight glowing on Mark Watson's orchids, 'because I have some flowers to paint.'

'Now look, Katherine,' said Vera sharply, 'I hope you're not going to make any trouble—?'

'And after that,' said Kate calmly, 'I'm going to go and buy myself a bikini. Goodbye, Vera.'

She replaced the receiver without waiting for an answer, and stalked out of her front door, slamming it behind her. Within a few minutes she was striding across Wimbledon Common, her blood still racing with anger. What a little cat Vera could be! Well, this time Vera was not going to get her own way. She stopped, watching a pair of rabbits scampering away in front of her. It had taken Vera's arrogant assumptions about Carlo Castelli to awaken Kate to her true feelings about him. She was *not* indifferent to him. She had been a fool to think so!

She walked towards one of her favourite spots on the Common, a large clump of prickly gorse which concealed a little nest of grass where one could shelter from the wind and others' eyes. The afternoon sun was warm, and she settled in her fortress of gorse on the sunlit grass. Carlo had done something to her. She knew now that she could never have let him simply walk out of her life. Antagonistic though their relations had been, Carlo Castelli had touched her in a way that no man had ever done. Nor was it simply his boundless masculinity which had captivated her; she was certain that her feeling for him—whatever it was—rose above simple desire.

She lay back, and gazed up into the clouds that were blowing across London. In the distance, the happy shouts

of two children drifted on the wind. Mark Watson's words
came into her mind suddenly. She *was* letting life pass her
by. Was she going to live for ever in her prickly little
sanctuary, sheltered from all the experiences of life?
Perhaps she had been so badly hurt when her parents had
died that she had retreated into herself too much. To think
of that day even now brought a lump to her throat. Yet five
long, lonely years had passed since then. Was it not time
now to emerge into the world once again? She thought of
the deep green in Carlo's eyes that night on the Thames;
and then of his powerful, mature presence at Claridges,
the way he had glanced at her when he had finished
speaking. Her skin rose in gooseflesh, and she rolled over.
Yes, he was ruthless—a man of the present, hard and
thrusting in his ways. And she knew that she was not
ready for him. That when next those glowing eyes met
hers, she would curl up, hedgehog-like, as she had always
done. Well, that could not be helped. Fate had tied her to
Carlo Castelli's chariot wheels—and she was bound to
follow him.

She arose out of her nest and began to walk back to her
flat. A flame of excitement had begun to flicker in her
heart. She would tackle Mark's orchids later—for now,
she was going shopping!

Eight days later she was walking across the tarmac to an
Alitalia jet, whose roaring engines were already filling the
air with the smell of excitement. Kate glanced up at the
mighty engines poised above her, wondering as she always
did how so vast a mechanism could ever fly; and then she
was walking up the aluminium ladder, carrying her bag in
one hand and a light coat in the other.

As she settled into her seat, struggling with the safety-

belt, she could not suppress a shiver of nervous antici-
pation. Carlo and Vera would already be on their way to
Leparú. Carlo had left London days before, to settle his
management affairs in preparation for his long holiday in
Sicily. Kate had seen him only once, briefly, before he had
left. All he had said to her had been, 'I am glad you are
coming, Caterina; I will see you in Leparú.' She had been
too confused, too disturbed at parting, to meet his eyes;
like a fool, she had turned and run, wordlessly.

And Vera had left a day earlier. Since the day Kate had
phoned her to say she had decided not to go to Leparú,
Vera had maintained a frigid silence towards her. Mentally, Kate shrugged her shoulders. Vera was capable of
extremely childish behaviour. And as for what was going to
happen between Vera and Carlo—Kate closed her mind
resolutely to the subject. For once in her life she was going
to allow things to simply evolve. She had taken that de-
cision. On Leparú, she was just going to let things happen.

She stowed her bag under her seat. Inside it were some
of the clothes she had bought for this holiday. Obeying
five years' accumulation of frugal instincts, she had shop-
ped at Marks and Spencers, Woolworth's, Boots, buying
simple cotton beachwear. But when it had come to her
bathing costumes, Kate had been unable to settle for
something economical and dull. With Uncle Roger's
legacy to urge her on, she had found a small shop in Bond
Street which had matched her own strict tastes. In the end
she had bought three costumes, whose total cost had
exceeded her rent for several months. Yet the extrava-
gance had been worth it. Of the two bikinis, she knew that
she would need unusual courage to wear the smallest—
two scraps of thin gold material which had looked so
ravishing on her pale, slender figure that she had scarcely

recognised herself in the dressing-cubicle mirror. The other was not much bigger, but the blue and crimson Lycra hugged her body less shamelessly, and she would feel less like Mata Hari in it. The third costume was her favourite. It was a sheer black one-piece, tailored with magical skill, low enough in the neckline and high enough at the hip to flatter her figure. It was a classic, elegant thing, in which she would feel superbly confident. And at the same boutique she had splashed out on two or three silk scarves, a long, simple dress, and four pairs of rather cheeky towelling shorts.

She watched the airport through the Perspex of the window, waiting for the take-off. Eventually everything was ready. The doors thumped shut, closing off the whine of the engines, and the dark, attractive stewardess was demonstrating the use of survival gear 'in the unlikely event of depressurisation' as the plane taxied to the take-off runway.

Kate found that a good-looking blond man had taken the seat next to her. He was smiling rather nervously at her, and she noticed that he was clutching his armrests tightly.

'Your first flight?' she asked, in answer to his polite greeting.

He nodded ruefully. 'Does it show?'

'Don't worry,' Kate smiled sympathetically. 'Everyone gets nervous at take-off.'

'I'm glad to hear it,' he said somewhat wanly. 'Are you stopping in Rome?'

'No, I'm going on to Sicily. And you?'

'I'm going to Siena, on business for my firm.' He stuck out a large hand, and Kate noticed that his wrist was covered in pale blond hairs. 'Peter Nicholls,' he said.

'Kate Melville.' She shook his hand.

'Is there any chance of this plane crashing?' he asked anxiously.

'None at all,' she told him with unfounded confidence. 'It never happens at Heathrow, anyway. And these Alitalia pilots are among the best in the business.'

'Really?' he asked, looking rather relieved.

'Really,' she assured him, secretly amused that such a big, strong man should be so nervous. Reassuring him had restored her own confidence, and she settled back to enjoy the take-off.

The roar of the engines rose to a deep throbbing howl as the jet began to accelerate along the runway. Almost dreamily, Kate watched the airfield whip past with blurring speed, as the acceleration thrust her back into her seat like a giant hand. Then the nose of the plane was up, and the rumble of the wheels was still. For a minute or two, the long cabin was at a forty-five-degree angle as the plane climbed steeply towards the sun, and then it began to level off slowly. With a little *ping* the NO SMOKING lights went off. Peter Nicholls let out his breath with a whoosh.

'By God,' he muttered, wiping his face, 'I thought we'd had it there!' He turned to Kate with a look of admiration. 'You're a pretty cool customer, Miss Melville. Can I buy you a drink?'

As the plane winged its way towards Rome, Kate fell into conversation with the young businessman. It turned out that he was a sales representative for a British computer firm. Intrigued, she asked him about Data-Castelli. He pulled a wry face.

'They're top dogs in Europe at the moment. Competing with them is sheer hell. They've got a superb reputation, and though I hate to admit it, their product is unbeat-able.'

Kate smiled.'It's very honest of you to say that.'

'Well, my firm makes a different series, so we aren't in competition all the time. Data-Castelli specialise in big machines—gigantic processors that deal with huge amounts of work for factories, city councils, govern-ments—that sort of thing. We do much smaller stuff—office calculators, adding-machines, that line of product.' He sipped from his gin and tonic.

'So Data-Castelli are big business?' she prompted.

'Oh, huge,' he said. 'It's a multi-million-pound cor-poration. Why do you ask?'

'I happened to meet Carlo Castelli some days ago—the head of the whole show.'

Peter Nicholls raised blond eyebrows.

'You must move in good company, Miss Melville. I'd give a lot to have met Carlo Castelli.'

'Is he good at his job?'

'He's outstanding,' confirmed the young salesman. 'He's got a brilliant grasp of computer science, to start with. He actually designed the basic Data-Castelli com-puter unit. And in the second place, he's got a wonderful sense of style. He knows how to promote a product like nobody else in the business—he leaves the local chaps miles behind.'

'Does he, indeed?' commented Kate, inwardly grin-ning. Though Peter Nicholls did not know it, she could confirm his praise of Carlo Castelli from personal experi-ence! For some reason, the man's unbiased praise of Carlo had warmed her heart. She gazed out of the window at the cloudland below, gilded with the late afternoon sun. It was a beautiful, dreamlike vista—you felt you could get out and walk on those soft cottonwool peaks so far below. The intercom pinged again for attention.

'In twenty minutes we shall be landing at Rome airport,' intoned the stewardess. 'We shall be beginning our descent shortly.' As the tiny buildings of Rome drifted into view thousands of feet below them, washed with the pale orange of the setting sun, Kate felt a fleeting regret that she was not staying in this great city. But there was Sicily to come!

During the landing Peter Nicholls, an old hand by now, was calm. In the arrivals lounge at the huge Fiumicino Airport, Kate waved goodbye to him, and made her way towards Domestic Departures. The flight had landed in perfect time, and there was no rush to make her connecting flight to Sicily.

Within an hour she was boarding another Alitalia flight, bound for Catania. By now she was conscious of being in Italy, with Italians. The other people on the flight were dark, elegantly dressed, full of that vivacity and poise that distinguishes Italy. Even the coffee that the smiling stewardess brought her was distinctive—dark and fragrantly strong. Hesitantly Kate began to use her rusty schoolgirl Italian, and was soon in conversation with the old lady next to her.

The sun had set, and the sky was a dark blue outside the Perspex windows of the cabin, so Kate saw nothing of her journey. At midnight exactly, the jet was touching down at Catania airport. The night air was warm as she walked across the apron towards the Immigration building. In the darkness, she could see the high mountains that surrounded the landing-field. Once through the formalities of arrival, she waited for her suitcases at the baggage terminal. Tiredness washed over her as she hefted the two

Revelation cases on to her trolley and trundled them through to the reception lounge. She was due to meet one of the staff from Leparú here, and as she looked around the half-empty hall, she caught sight of a short, plump man holding up a card reading *Caterina Melville*. When he saw her coming towards him, he waved vigorously, showing gold teeth in a welcoming smile.

'Signorina Melville? Welcome to Sicily.'

'Thank you,' she smiled, as he took her bags.

'My name is Rosario,' he told her, as he bustled a pathway for her out of the building. 'I am to take you to Leparú. Did you have a comfortable flight?'

'Yes, very pleasant, thanks. You speak good English, Rosario.'

'Signor Courtney taught me,' he said, then put down the suitcases with a sorrowing face. 'It was such a tragedy, *signorina*. We could all see that he was sick. But would he see the doctor? No, no, no. I've never known such a stubborn man as your uncle. But so kind, *signorina*—a saint, believe me.' He nodded several times, a woebegone expression on his cherubic, unshaven face, then took her bags up again, and led her to a waiting taxi. 'We are going down to the dock,' he explained, 'to get the boat to Leparú.'

As they drove through the night to the docks, Kate asked, 'Is Leparú far, Rosario?'

'No, only about fifteen miles from the coast,' he told her. 'You can see the mainland very clearly from Leparú.'

'People tell me it's very pretty,' she prompted.

'Oh, *signorina*—' Rosario made an eloquent gesture with one chubby hand, '—it's like Paradiso, believe me!'

At the wharf, he paid off the taxi, and hefted her luggage aboard a large motor-launch. By the neon lights of the lamp-posts, she could see that the name emblazoned on the hull was *Coco*. She smiled, recognising the name of a famous clown.

'I suppose this was Roger's boat?'

'Yes, this was the *padrone*'s boat, *signorina*.' He helped her aboard, started up the engines, and began to steer the boat out into the open sea. With a flash of memory Kate recalled that night on the Thames with Carlo, another boat sailing out into other waters.

'Have the others arrived yet, Rosario?'

'*Sì*—the Signorina de Cruz has been here since yesterday, and Signor Carlo has been here since two days ago.' The launch passed through the breakwater into the waves of the open Mediterranean. A cool, fresh, marine smell met Kate's nostrils, and she inhaled deeply. They left the lights of the harbour behind them, and the powerful boat cut through into the darkness ahead.

'Tell me a little about Leparú,' she asked Rosario as he held the wheel. 'Is there a lot of staff there?'

'Only four, *signorina*. I myself—then old Tomaso and Santino, who look after the island and the gardens between them, and Sara. She is my wife,' he grinned at Kate, 'but she is twice my size. Sara does all the housework and the washing. You must not argue with Sara,' he told her mock-solemnly, 'because she is plenty of woman!' Smiling, Kate left him to pilot the boat in peace, and went out to lean on the rail. The fresh sea-spray was clearing her head, lifting her tiredness a little, though she was by now ready for bed.

All excitement seemed to have faded now, and she was calm, resolved. Whatever lay ahead, she would meet it confidently. Over to the east, a smudge of grey heralded the coming dawn. She thought of the brilliance of that dawn on the Thames. Would the sun ever rise as brightly as that for her again?

'Not far now,' called Rosario. 'If you look ahead, you can see Leparú.'

Kate looked forward, and saw a dark hump against the horizon. Silhouetted against the silver of the coming dawn she thought she could see woods, a large hill.

'It looks very big,' she called back to Rosario.

His cherubic face nodded happily in the cabin light.

'It is quite big, *signorina*. There are lots of beautiful beaches. The *padrone* made it very pleasant while he was alive.'

The island was looming out of the darkness now. Rosario was steering the boat towards a long jetty which projected from a small natural cove. Kate could see a wide beach, and a slipway. Above it, steps climbed steeply up to a large terrace overlooking the sea. And as the boat chugged slowly to moor at the jetty, she could see a tall figure waiting with folded arms on the edge of the planking. It was Carlo.

CHAPTER SIX

His embrace was quick and forceful.

'Welcome to Leparú, Caterina,' he said softly into her ear, then helped Rosario to moor the launch to a stanchion. Kate watched his lithe figure in the darkness, her heart beating fast. When he came to take her arm, she caught the glint of his smile.

'Are you tired?'

'Not too bad—I could do with a few hours' sleep.'

'You can lie on the beach all morning,' he told her, leading her up the stone stairs to the terrace. The coming dawn showed a long, beautiful villa stretched out on the slope above the beach. Fronted by a long balustraded verandah, it looked over the sea serenely in the pale blue light. Carlo led her through the front door into the darkened house, along a corridor, and to a bedroom facing the sea.

'This will be your bedroom,' he said, as Rosario put down her bags, and bade them a smiling goodnight. 'You can explore it all in the morning,' he smiled. By the bedside light, his eyes were tawny-gold, and his almost shockingly handsome face was calm. He patted her cheek gently, then let himself out, closing the bedroom door behind him.

Stupid with tiredness, Kate looked about her. The bedroom was large and airy, furnished with a simple yet exquisite taste which surprised her. She had expected Roger's house to be fantastic, bizarre. She had not been prepared for the elegance of this cool white furniture, the

very beautiful materials of curtain and bedspread, the
opulent rugs on the floor, the sandalwood cupboards that
scented the whole room. Leading off to the right was a
red-tiled shower. Past it was a large bathroom, with one of
the biggest baths Kate had ever seen. She gaped at it,
fascinated. It was made of black marble, and the taps were
burnished brass. She looked around. The tiles were hand-
painted, and the floor had been covered with a thick pile
carpet, thoughtfully made for wet, bare feet.

Amazed, she walked back into the bedroom, this time
noticing the charming little chandelier that hung from the
ceiling, the watercolours that hung on the walls. This was
a woman's room, she decided, cool, elegant, and beautiful. Who had it been furnished for? On a little ebony table,
among a collection of pretty shells, stood a photograph of
Roger Courtney. She picked it up, gazing down into the
lined, smiling face of the uncle she had not seen since
childhood. 'Poor Roger,' she whispered softly. She put the
silver-framed photograph on her bedside table, deciding
to unpack in the morning. She kicked off her sandals
wearily, took off the clothes she had worn for the journey,
and clad only in her pants, slipped between the cool
sheets, exhausted. Her last thought was of Carlo's hard
embrace, and then her mind slipped into the depths of
sleep.

Despite her weariness, Kate slept only a few hours, and
awoke refreshed. The villa was silent, and she lay in bed
for a few minutes, listening to the sound of the sea through
the half-open window. Finally, unable to lie in bed any
longer, she jumped up, and went over to the window. The
sky was a magnificent clear blue. It was only seven-thirty,
and the sun was already climbing steadily to the meridian.
And the sea! It was a colour Kate had never dreamed

of—a deep ultramarine, with turquoise glints, as transparent as tinted glass. Her heart rising with joy, Kate decided that she must go down for an early morning swim. Hastily she rummaged through her suitcases until she found what she wanted, the little gold bikini and a white towelling dress. Slipping the minuscule costume on, she covered herself with the cool dress, slipped her feet into sandals, and picking up a towel, emerged cautiously from her bedroom. As she walked down the corridor, a woman was sweeping in the sitting-room ahead. She was quite short, but extremely plump, with an enormous, comfortable bosom, and a merry face.

'You must be Sara,' Kate smiled.

The woman grinned, showing white teeth, and nodded like her husband.

'*Io sono Sara*,' she affirmed. 'No speaka good English, *signorina*.'

'That's all right,' said Kate, charmed by her Southern smile. '*Io vado alla spiaggia*—I'm going for a swim.'

The plump woman nodded happily, waving her hand at the direction to take. 'Later—I bring breakfast,' she said. As she walked through the long sitting-room to the wide French doors, Kate decided that she was going to enjoy staying on Leparú!

The sitting-room was as beautifully furnished as her own bedroom had been. The smooth stone floor, obviously the original floor of the old building, had been strewn with Persian rugs. The furniture was sturdily practical for a beachside villa, yet stylish and attractive nonetheless—wide-cushioned in some pretty, flowered material. The walls were hung with paintings, painted tiles, the green glass floats which local fishermen used on their nets, some beautifully-shaped pieces of wood from old spinning-wheels and hand-ploughs, a set of brass harness-buckles—a delightful and eccentric collection of objects. From the resinous beams of the roof, bunches of dried herbs hung down, filling the room with a faint, pleasing aromatic smell. It was a spacious, charming room, made to live in and be enjoyed.

She walked through the fragrant lemon-grove down to the sea, sniffing the air appreciatively. In the distance, a man was picking oranges. He gave her a cheery wave, and she waved back, guessing that this would be either Tomaso or Santino.

The beach itself was like something out of a dream, white and incredibly clean. The purple shape of Sicily was visible across the sunlit sea, and the tiny triangles of a few yacht sails drifted in the early morning breeze. The sand was deliciously warm between her toes, and she dropped her clothes on her outspread towel against a friendly sand-dune, and scampered down to the water in her tiny gold bikini.

The sea had not yet had time to warm in the sun yet, and it was wonderfully cool against her skin. Joyously, she plunged into the water and submerged her pale body in its ultramarine depths. As she floated, entranced, among the gentle waves, she turned to look back at Leparú. The villa set on the hills was beautiful—perfectly matching its wonderful setting. Its walls were the colour of vanilla ice-cream, and the long orange roof was intricately tiled. It stood on its lawn, behind the lemon grove, looking down on to the sea.

The cool water bobbed Kate gently in its arms. Signs of life were stirring in the villa. A little trickle of smoke appeared momentarily at one of the chimneys—a stove being lighted, she guessed—and two figures appeared at the French doors. She rolled on to her stomach and paddled towards a group of smooth grey rocks, covered with spongy seaweed. She hauled herself out of the water and drew her knees up on the warm perch, gazing back at the long shape of Sicily. The white cone to the west, she guessed, must be Etna. A tiny white plume at its tip confirmed her guess. She peered down into the water that swirled around her rock. It was an unbelievable blue, and as clear as bathwater. She could see tiny fish darting in the blue depths, and the sandy bottom was strewn with shells and pebbles.

A little piece of paradise indeed! Happier than she had been for weeks, Kate slipped back into the cool water and swam to shore. The welcoming warmth of the beach lulled her into a delicious sleepiness. Adjusting her bikini, she lay face-down on her dry towel, and closed her eyes. The sun was a giant, hot caress on her back, and she felt her body relaxing, like melting butter.

She was aroused by the sound of Vera's clear voice, answered by Carlo's deep laugh. They were walking towards her, and she stiffened with resentment for a moment, and decided to feign sleep. She lay with her head on one side, her eyes tightly closed, and listened to them approaching.

'Ah,' purred Carlo's voice, 'I see one of the mermaids has fallen asleep on the beach.'

'So I see,' came Vera's cool tones. 'Did she arrive last night?'

'Yes—I went down to the jetty to meet her at two a.m.'

'You're too kind to that girl,' said Vera disapprovingly. Then her voice changed to the saccharine coo of a turtle-dove. 'Would you be an *angel*, Carlo, and help me with this zip? It seems to be stuck.'

There was a pause, then the sound of a zip being undone. And then a little coy shriek from Vera, followed by her flirtatious giggle. It was difficult for Kate to stop her toes from curling with fury. She listened to the sounds of Carlo and Vera settling down next to her, trying to keep her breathing even.

'Isn't it heavenly?' came Vera's fluting voice.

'Mmm. Are you glad you came?'

'Oh, definitely. I can't tell you how glad I am,' came Vera's voice, heavy with meaning. Then her voice changed again. 'She's a bit under-dressed, don't you think?'

'I don't think so,' purred Carlo's deep voice. 'It's a beautiful costume, is it not?'

'It's very *small*,' said Vera. 'Probably came from Woolworth's. For an artist, Kate has decidedly plebeian tastes.'

'Oh, I disagree,' said Carlo, and Kate could hear the smile in his voice. 'I'd say that costume didn't cost under a hundred pounds. It's a work of art.'

'A miniature, then.'

'If you like. Besides, a figure like that deserves to be shown off.'

'Do you think she's pretty?' Vera asked casually, but with a ripple of jealousy under the smooth tone. 'I think she's rather skinny, myself. Carlo, sweetie, could you rub some cream into my back?'

Kate lay still, listening with rising indignation to Vera's barely-suppressed sighs of delight as Carlo rubbed the sun-tan lotion into her back. Really, Vera was shameless! She was behaving like a cat in heat!

'No, I don't agree,' came Carlo's calm voice. 'I've always thought Kate's figure was rather voluptuous. The slender look is simply because she's so well proportioned. But look how fine her skin is.'

'Hmm,' said Vera, somewhat bitterly.

'And she has rather splendid hips, don't you think?'

'I don't know,' said Vera shortly.

'Oh yes—quite perfectly shaped. Womanly, without being heavy. And she has a delightful bottom, too. Look at the way her thighs taper so elegantly down to her knees—like a courtesan in a Bronzino painting. As for her calves—'

The blush that was washing into Kate's cheeks made all pretence at sleep ridiculous. Hearing her body so minutely described by Carlo was incredibly embarrassing! She raised herself up on one elbow, pink-cheeked, and glared at him. The mocking smile on the bold mouth told her that she had fallen for one of his wicked jokes.

'Ah,' he purred, 'Sleeping Beauty awakes!'

'We were just talking about you, Katherine,' said Vera coolly.

'I know,' retorted Kate. 'I heard you.' She sat up, dusting sand from her knees, and studied them. Vera was wearing a vivid lime-green bikini that showed her rather full figure off well. Carlo, who was lying on his back, half-raised on his elbows, was wearing only a narrow black bathing costume. His body was stunningly beautiful. The way he was lying had brought his stomach muscles into relief, taut and hard under his velvety, golden skin. His broad chest was covered with a wide triangle of sparkling black hair that tapered down on to his belly and disappeared into his costume. His grey-green eyes surveyed her with calm arrogance over his magnificent body, and Kate met them with a sense of shock. She always tended to forget quite how splendid

Carlo was, how vivid his physical presence could be. Suddenly, she wished that he were not so scantily clad. That body was too beautiful to be shown off—it should be concealed, away from the hungry eyes of other women. And she began to regret having worn such a tiny costume herself. The gold material was wickedly thin, and her own body had responded in no uncertain terms to the direct-ness of his gaze. She could feel the skin on her breasts tautening under this thin material, and folded her arms hastily. But not before his eyes had dropped to them, and detected the unambiguous signals that her nipples had made. The smile on his face widened naughtily, and his eyes met hers again with an emerald sparkle before taking in the rest of her body with calm interest.

'You'd better not get too much sun today, Katherine,' said Vera acidly. 'Your skin is very white, and you'll burn yourself to a crisp. Perhaps you'd better put a shirt on.'

'I think I will,' said Kate shortly. She rummaged in her basket, and pulled on a cotton T-shirt over her torso. What had possessed her to buy that tiny bikini in the first place? She sat crosslegged, looking out to sea, her side turned resentfully to Carlo.

'We're being pampered this morning,' he said. 'Here comes Sara with some breakfast.'

Sara had arrived with a large tray full of fruit and a steaming percolator which breathed out the fragrance of fresh coffee. She said something in the Sicilian dialect to Carlo.

'She wants you to know that all the fruit is grown on Leparú,' he explained. He held up a magnificent yellow peach. 'Peaches, tangerines, oranges, pears—the fruits of paradise.' He poured coffee for them all, and passed a dainty little cup to each. 'So you've had a swim already?' he asked Kate smoothly. 'What's your first impression of Leparú?'

'It's beautiful,' she said sincerely. 'I've never seen a lovelier spot than this. And the beach is so clean!'

'We can explore the whole island later on,' he smiled. 'There's more to see besides the beach.'

'It must be worth all of a quarter of a million,' said Vera loudly. 'Surely it can't sell for less?'

'Perhaps not,' Carlo shrugged.

'I'm sure of it,' persisted Vera. 'From what I've seen of it, there should be quite a queue of people waiting to buy it.'

Kate gulped down her coffee, suddenly disgusted by Vera's mercenary instincts.

'I'm going for a walk,' she announced, and without looking at either of them, stalked off along the beach. Somehow, she was absolutely certain that Carlo's eyes would be on her legs, and she felt her face reddening as she walked.

'Really!' she heard Vera say. She trotted down to the waterline and walked along the edge of the waves, up to her ankles in the cool, foaming water. About two hundred yards from the others, she turned and looked back. Vera was lying ecstatically on her brown tummy, while Carlo rubbed suntan lotion into the backs of her thighs. Angrily, Kate turned away, and stalked on. The beach was endlessly beautiful before her.

She walked for about twenty minutes, picking up the prettiest shells she could find, until her fists were full of their smooth, sharp-edged shapes. By some black rocks, she settled down in the sand to examine her treasure-trove. She laid the shells out into little groups, and studied their lovely patterns absently. Why was she always so gauche with Carlo? She did not care about Vera, but she was furious with herself for having behaved like a child, yet again, in front of Carlo.

If ever she had wanted to be cool and confident, it was now. Carlo Castelli was not the sort of man who would be amused by clumsiness. Why could she never retain her poise in his presence? Was it simply a matter of sex-appeal? Or did he really stir her emotions? She pushed her shells around with an idle forefinger, remembering the velvety smoothness of his skin. She knew from experience that the softness of his skin covered muscles like supple steel. She remembered the thin black bathing costume with a twinge of anger. It was shamelessly small! He had no right to show off his wonderful body in front of Vera.

She looked up with a start. Carlo was strolling across the sand towards her, carrying her towel. She sat back on the sand to await him, her heart thudding.

He moved with the unconscious grace of a panther, long legs carrying him with smooth power. His was a man's body, Kate thought, not a boy's—it was hard, balanced. She wondered how many women it had known, how many had gazed at its strength and beauty with the same wonder she now felt.

'You left your breakfast behind,' he said as he came up to her. He was holding a large pink-and-yellow peach in his free hand.

'Where's my cousin Vera?' she asked coolly.

'She fell asleep in the sun,' he smiled. 'And I thought a walk would do me good, so I've been following in your footsteps. Literally.' He held out the peach. 'Hungry? I'll go and wash it for you.' He stepped down to the edge of the

sea, and rinsed the fruit in the frothing water, then
brought it back to her.

'Thank you, *signor*.'

She bit into its softness. The salt of the sea-water on its
surface made a piquant contrast to the nectar sweetness of
the flesh. Carlo sighed, and stretched out lithe brown
arms.

'This is Eden,' he said. 'I was getting cramped, stuck in
my office all day long. A man gets cooped up in this
modern world. Men were made to tread the earth and
swim the sea, not to sit at desks, crouching over tele-
phones.'

'Yet you once told me you were a man of the present,'
she said, between mouthfuls of the luscious peach.

He smiled. 'This *is* the present, Caterina. Is your peach
sweet?'

'Delicious,' she said, wiping juice from her chin with
her wrist.

His tawny eyes watched her wet mouth for an instant,
then flicked up to look into her own eyes. 'You seem tense,
cara.'

'I'm perfectly relaxed,' she told him.

He looked up to watch three gulls drifting on the breeze
overhead. 'Why are you so hostile, Caterina? Every move
I have made towards being friends with you has been a
disaster. Do you hate me?'

'I'm indifferent to you,' she said, meeting his mocking
smile defiantly. 'Why do you laugh at me? Is it so unusual
for a woman to be indifferent to Carlo Castelli?'

'Oh, not unusual at all,' he said, his laughter rumbling
in his chest.

'Then what's so funny?' she demanded.

'You are, my dear.'

'Why?'

'Do you know,' he said gently, 'that under this sky, your eyes are violet? It's very striking.'

'Is that what makes you laugh, *signor?*'

With terrifying swiftness, he scooped her up in his arms, with as little effort as if she had been a cat. Kate screamed, kicking her legs helplessly, as he carried her down to the sea.

'Let me go!' she gasped, struggling against his hard muscles.

He stared down into her face with dancing eyes. 'If you do not begin calling me Carlo from this moment onwards,' he said calmly, 'I am going to drown you.'

'Put me down!'

He walked steadily into the waves, and dropped her into the cool water. As she resurfaced, spluttering, he ducked her head under the water again. She came up in panic.

'Have your own way,' she gurgled angrily. 'Carlo, Carlo, Carlo! Does that satisfy you?'

'If you ever call me Signor Castelli again,' he told her, 'I am going to bring you back to this same piece of beach, and drown you in the sea. Do you believe me?'

'I believe you!' she yelped, as wet, strong arms reached for her again.

'Come on, then—let's swim out to those rocks.'

Kate followed him through the water to the line of seal-like rocks. He swam with an easy, efficient Australian crawl, the water surging over his golden back. He was at the rocks long before her, and as she swam up, he took her hands in his own and pulled her up on to the slippery surface. Sitting next to him, she pulled her hair free of the elastic loop with which she had tied it into a ponytail, and

shook the golden waves loose, before tying it back again.
He watched her movements with bright eyes.

'Your hair is lovely,' he said. 'Why do you never wear it
loose?'

'Don't I?' she said in some surprise. 'I suppose it's
because I've never bothered to have it cut into any sort of a
style.'

'You should bother,' he smiled, tugging a lock of it
playfully. 'It's thick and beautiful, and such a rich gold
colour. If you are not careful, the sun and the sea will
bleach it bone-white.'

She pulled her hair back in silence, and secured it into
an untidy ponytail. Carlo shook his head mockingly. 'I am
going to the mainland tomorrow morning,' he said. 'I
have to see somebody in Catania. If you like, I'll take you
to see where Roger is buried. And there are some good
hairdressers in the city, too. We can get your hair cut into
something better than the dead poodle look.'

'That would be nice,' she said stiffly. 'Hadn't you better
be getting back now? Vera will be missing you, I'm sure.'

'She will be distressed by now,' he agreed. 'Are you
jealous of Vera, my dear Kate?'

'Of course not,' she snapped, and slipped off her perch
back into the sea. 'I'm going ashore,' she called over her
shoulder.

'I'll race you,' he grinned, plunging in like a golden
dolphin behind her.

Lunch, though delicious, was a strained affair. Vera's
expression told Kate quite plainly what she thought of
Carlo's little walk along the beach to find her. And Kate
herself was tense and moody. Carlo alone seemed un-
affected, making conversation with the well-bred grace he

possessed in such abundance. The last thing Kate wanted
to do was to get involved in some kind of a competition for
Carlo's attention with Vera. She glanced at Vera's pretty,
sullen face with a sinking heart. This was no way to begin
a holiday. As if reading her mind, Carlo leaned back in his
chair.

'Let's go for a stroll this afternoon. There are some
lovely spots on the island, and perhaps I can show the two
of you round them?'

The two women assented with little enthusiasm, and
after coffee, they all walked up past the villa towards the
hill that lay at the centre of the island.

The vegetation was fascinating, thought Kate, a
strange mixture of Africa and Europe, of wildness and
cultivation. Palm trees and cycads grew alongside lemon
trees and the gnarled wild olive. The grass was springy
and dry under their feet, and the paved pathway was
bordered on either side with an abundance of wild flowers.
The scarlet poppies caught Kate's eyes especially, and she
gathered an armful as she went, intending to paint them
later.

She also found a little group of wild cyclamens growing
under a little oak. They were bigger, and more violet-hued
than the one Carlo had picked for her in England. She
took one, and tucked it defiantly into her hair. Vera
noticed this little bit of vanity with a sour smile, but
Carlo's expression did not change. Had he forgotten
already?

At the top of the hill, they paused for breath, looking
down the long slope to the red roof of the villa, and the
blue sea that curled white on to the beach below. The
island was more extensive than Kate had imagined. It was
the shape of an uneven wedge, tapering down to beaches

at one end, but rising up steadily to end in quite steep cliffs at the other. Kate guessed it to be about six miles long.

'It's volcanic, of course,' Carlo told them. 'This whole area was—still is—the seat of volcanic activity. Only Etna is still going strong, but on some of the other islands there are hot springs and sulphur baths. It was volcanoes which brought all these islands, including Sicily itself, up from the sea-bed.'

He led them along the path, which had now become a wild track amongst the flowers, towards a little valley. It was a picturesque spot, lush and green, shaded with a large copse of ilex trees. The grass was brilliant with wild flowers, and the little meadow ended at the edge of a steep precipice, which dropped clear down to the sea, some hundreds of feet below. Kate stared down the edge of the cliff, watching the sea crawling amongst the rocks, so far away. Gulls wheeled below them, and now and then the wind blew the faint rumble of the sea up to them.

'Leparú has been inhabited since prehistoric times,' said Carlo. 'There were stone-age people here—Roger found a lot of their flints and obsidian arrowheads. This spot was a sacred grove in ancient times.'

'You mean they used to sacrifice here?' asked Vera, looking around the copse as though she half expected to see a naked savage emerge from the trees.

'Well,' Carlo smiled, 'they used to worship here. Their altar was that rock, where Kate is sitting.'

Kate looked at the oddly-shaped boulder with new interest.

'It does seem to have been shaped,' she said. 'There's a little hollow here.'

Carlo nodded. 'That's where they would have sacrificed, or perhaps simply laid offerings of milk or fruit. In later times, the Greeks colonised Leparú, and they used this place as a temple too. If you look carefully, you'll find fragments of pottery around—maybe even whole pots, and bits of bronze and ivory.'

'You mean—treasure?' asked Vera, her eyes glowing.

'If you like,' he smiled. 'You're unlikely to find any gold or silver, but you might find something of interest if you look around. Shall we have a search?'

Eagerly they began to hunt through the pebbles and broken rock around the site. Even Vera seemed to have entered into the spirit of the search. Soon they were turning up pieces of painted clay, and Vera screamed with delight when she picked up two bronze arrowheads. Suddenly Kate spotted something made of terracotta, half buried in the gravel. Carefully she scraped the sand away from it and picked it up. It was a little clay vessel with a handle, and two holes in the top, shaped like an old-fashioned candle-holder. She could just make out some kind of pattern painted around the holes. She took it to show Carlo.

He clapped his hands softly. 'Well done,' he said. 'That's an oil-lamp—Greek, by the look of it. You must have sharp eyes, Caterina—I've scoured this place many times, and I've never found anything as nice as this.'

Vera had come up, and was looking at the little object resentfully.

'It's very ordinary,' she said drily.

'It's well over two thousand years old,' Carlo told her. 'Sometimes these things have little patterns underneath.' He turned the oil-lamp over and brushed sand away from the bottom. In the terracotta, a little figure of a man had been carved with considerable delicacy. He had goat's legs, and was playing a double flute. They crowded round to look at it more closely.

'It's a satyr,' Carlo smiled. 'An ancient Greek fertility symbol.'

'I see what you mean,' said Vera with a giggle.

Puzzled, Kate looked closer, and then a blush suffused her face. The little figure was undoubtedly male—the artist had emphasised that most plainly!

'Well, I never,' said Vera. 'What a wicked little drawing!'

'Caterina,' said Carlo, his deep voice amused, 'I believe you're blushing!'

'You take the thing,' she said, pushing it away in embarrassment. 'I don't want it.'

'Oh, no—you must keep it. It will bring you luck. If Sara knew you'd found one of these, she'd be delighted.'

'Why?'

'It means you'll be getting married shortly,' he grinned, offering her the lamp. She shook her head, her cheeks still warm, but he took her hand and placed the little thing in her palm closing her fingers around it. 'I'm not teasing you,' he said, his beautiful eyes intent on hers. 'It will bring you luck. Keep it.'

The lamp was cool and light in her hand. She thrust it into her pocket, confused, and began to walk back down the path towards the house. Carlo and Vera followed her. She picked up her bunch of poppies where she had lain them, and set off ahead.

She was deep in thought when Vera fell into step beside her.

'What was that crack about getting married soon supposed to mean?' Vera enquired coldly. Kate glanced at her in surprise.

'It's probably a local superstition, or something,' she shrugged.

Vera snorted. '"Or something" is right! What are you and that man cooking up between you?'

'No one's cooking up anything, Vera.'

'You promised to stay away from Carlo Castelli, Katherine.'

'As a matter of fact, I didn't,' Kate replied coolly. 'But in any case, I've been trying to get away from both of you all morning, in case you haven't noticed.'

'Really? Then what made you wear that *shameless* bikini this morning? You looked positively pornographic!'

'Your confection in green wasn't much bigger,' Kate pointed out gently. 'And I had no idea you were going to come and join me there.'

'Indeed?' snapped Vera. 'Well, you didn't lose any time in spiriting Castelli away, did you? And what were you discussing on your so-called walk?'

'We didn't talk about anything,' replied Kate in exasperation.

'Too busy cuddling in the sand, I suppose? Don't try and tell me you haven't been conspiring with Castelli behind my back, Katherine. And there's another thing— what's the idea behind this secret expedition to Catania tomorrow? Why wasn't I invited?'

'Carlo simply wants to show me Roger's grave, Vera. And I want to get my hair done, that's all.'

'Yes—you'll want to look your ravishing best,' the other woman sneered.

'If you're so worried about our trip to Catania tomorrow, why don't you come along?'

'And play gooseberry?' Vera snapped. 'No, thank you!'

'Listen, Vera.' Kate turned to face her with angry eyes. 'You can get one thing straight right now—I'm not going to marry Carlo for the sake of a half-share in Leparú. I told you once before, I'm not that sort of person.'

'Of course not,' sneered Vera. 'You want the whole thing, don't you?'

'What do you mean by that?'

'I know what your game is—you're hoping to get Castelli infatuated with you, so he'll marry *you*, and not me—and then you'll have Leparú all to yourself!'

'For heaven's sake!'

'Don't look so innocent, Katherine. I remember what you said in London that day—it's illegal to make a contract to agree to divorce someone before you're married. You want to cut me out of my share of Roger's will.'

'Would it make any difference if I swore I had no such thoughts?'

'You could try,' said Vera petulantly.

'Vera, I swear I have no intention of cutting you out of your share of the inheritance. I'm here on holiday, and when the holday's over I'm going back to Wimbledon. If Carlo decides to marry you, then as far as I'm concerned, you can keep the whole island to yourself. The whole idea of marrying someone for money, and divorcing him afterwards, just sickens me!'

Vera stared into Kate's eyes for a minute.

'I wish I could believe you,' she said slowly. 'But somehow, I feel it in my bones that something's brewing between you and Castelli.'

'Not as far as I know, Vera. But I promise you that even if there is, I'd never keep you away from anything that's rightfully yours.'

'You'd better be serious about that, Katherine, or—'
Carlo's voice broke into Vera's sentence as he strolled up
to them.

'Can you hear that nightingale?' he asked, cocking his
head. He listened to the silence gravely for a minute. 'No,'
he said solemnly, 'your gay chatter must have frightened
it away. Let's go back for some tea.'

They walked down to the villa in silence. As they
were coming through the lemon grove, Carlo stopped
to pick one of the redolent fruit. He turned to face Vera
and **Kate**. His eyes were iceberg-green and emotion-
less.

'I couldn't help overhearing a part of your argument,'
he said drily. 'You weren't making much of a secret about
it.' His face was formidable. 'Let's get one thing clear,
ladies. Our holiday on this island is purely a business
arrangement.'

Kate and Vera both began to speak together, but Carlo
silenced them both with a cutting motion of his hand. 'I
don't want to hear any arguments from either of you. I
want some peace while I'm on Leparú. There will be no
conspiring, no arguing, no haggling, while I'm around. Is
that clear?' His cold eyes raked across them both. They
nodded, both considerably pale. 'I made an offer at
Claridges some days ago—that offer still stands. Nor will I
deviate from it by one iota. Is *that* clear?'

'Carlo,' began Kate, 'the whole plan horrifies me. I just
want to tell you that—'

'Please.' He cut through her sentence with a cold smile.
'Spare me the moral lectures, Katherine—save your ser-
mons for someone else. I'm not interested. Nor,' he added,
turning his icy gaze to Vera, 'am I interested in listening to
anyone's paranoid suspicions.' He tossed the fruit in his

hand, waiting for his words to sink in. Then his bold mouth curved into the old mocking smile. 'Now,' he said, 'shall we go and enjoy ourselves?'

CHAPTER SEVEN

As the motor-launch sped across the glittering water towards Catania the next day, Kate wondered for the hundredth time what it was that made her behave so clumsily with Carlo Castelli. The previous evening had not been a success. After Carlo's lecture in the lemon grove, both women were subdued; but while Vera had possessed the smooth charm to make conversation, and pull herself out of her gloom, Kate had remained tongue tied the whole evening. Over the games of Scrabble which Carlo had easily won, Kate had been gauche and shy, her emotions in a turmoil. She hated to think that Carlo could be so flippant and pragmatic about marriage. She glanced at him as he held the wheel, guiding the boat through the dancing waves, and realized that she knew very little about him. She determined to find out something of his childhood and his grandmother today.

Carlo docked *Coco* at the wharf, and they took a taxi to the garage where he was having his own car looked after. It was a pearl-grey Lancia, like the one he had hired in London—a beautiful car, but surprisingly un-flashy for a man of his wealth and power.

'I like to drive,' he smiled, as he edged the car out of its parking bay and waved to the attendant. 'I'm not interested in status symbols—I could never have a Mercedes or a Rolls. I like the power and lightness of this car, the elegance of its design. It appeals to my aesthetic sense.'

'I didn't know you designed your own computers,' Kate

ventured, as Carlo drove out into the downtown traffic.

'Have you been doing a little background research?' he asked, his smoky eyes catching her face with disconcerting amusement. 'Yes—I have a doctorate in computer design from Rome University.'

'Really? You did tell me once you were a scientist.'

'That was an interesting occasion,' he smiled, and Kate shrank into her seat with embarrassment, cursing herself for having brought that subject up. Carlo stopped the Lancia to buy some dark red roses. And as he slipped back behind the wheel, Kate asked, 'You told me you met Roger through your cousin Lydia—where does she live?'

'Lydia lives in Palermo, about fifty miles away,' he told her. 'She is a true Sicilian, but I am a cosmopolitan.'

'You're very Italian,' Kate ventured.

'I love Italy,' he nodded, his strong, competent hands guiding the car through the tangle of the traffic. 'But Sicily has always been more of a holiday home to me, even though I was born here.'

'Where did you grow up?' she prompted.

'In Rome. My grandmother took me there when I was still a baby.'

'Tell me about her.'

'Graziana Castelli,' he smiled reminiscently. 'She was a holy terror! She could tell you stories that would make your hair stand on end. She had once been a very famous singer; and even when I knew her, in her seventies, she was capable of beautiful singing.'

'You told me she sang before the Tzar.'

'Yes—she knew everybody, the Tzar of Russia, the King of Italy, the King of England. She was much admired by Theodore Roosevelt. When I was a little boy, all sorts of famous old men would still be coming to visit my grandmother. Generals, poets, statesmen—every-body. There was even a cardinal, I remember, who was infatuated with her, despite his own white hairs! Once, I remember, Pablo Picasso came to pay his respects, with his latest French girl-friend. And once Charles de Gaulle came, with a huge bunch of lilies.'

'It must have been very exciting for a little boy,' Kate said in awe.

Carlo grimaced, driving up towards an extensive, cypress-lined cemetery.

'Nonna was a grand old woman,' he said, 'but she was very harsh. She brought me up in a hard school. My childhood was very lonely, despite all the excitement of Nonna's visitors.'

'Is she still alive?'

'No. She died when I was seventeen. By then I was a man already.'

'I can imagine,' Kate murmured, but Carlo did not notice. He parked the Lancia, and together they walked between the long rows of marble tombstones in the bright Sicilian sunlight.

Roger's grave was simple and impressive—a flat marble slab bearing only his name and the dates of his birth and death. Curiously moved, Kate stared down at the pale stone, feeling a lump rising in her throat. Carlo put the bunch of roses silently into her hands, and she laid the flowers on Roger's tomb.

'Roger was a good man,' Carlo said gently. 'I think I was his only friend in his last years. You and I, Caterina, were the only two people in the world he cared anything about. Apart from his beloved Leparú.'

'Why wasn't he buried there?' she asked quietly.

'He didn't want it,' Carlo answered. He stood in silence

for a few minutes, then turned and walked slowly towards
another grave further away; an older and more opulent
affair, flanked by two lichen-covered angels and a little
flower-bed. Kate joined him quietly, and read the ornate
inscription. The finely-chiselled letters announced that
ETTORE BALDASARE DI MAGGIO CASTELLI
was buried here with his wife VITTORIA MARIA.

'Your parents?' she whispered. Carlo nodded. He had
kept a single red rose from the bunch he had bought, and
now he laid it in front of the tomb. Kate's eyes had misted
over, but Carlo's golden face was calm.

'I hope they are happy, wherever they are,' he said.
'Don't look so sad, Caterina—they died for love. And
besides, it was all a long time ago.' Suddenly he grinned,
and the tawny emerald eyes glinted. 'Well, now you know
how old I am,' he said. 'Let's go and get your hair cut.'

She emerged from the fantastically expensive salon an
hour and a half later, wondering whether it had all been
worth it. Carlo was due to pick her up in a few minutes,
and she studied herself in the mirror while she waited.
That morning she had chosen a simple cotton dress she
had bought in Bond Street, guessing that its severe elegance would be more appropriate than light holiday
attire. The hairdresser had cropped her golden hair quite
short, leaving a fringe across her high forehead, but letting
it drop in a burnished wave around her ears and the back
of her neck. It was undoubtedly a very sophisticated cut.
She tried an experimental turn of the head, and the
golden hair swung lightly back into place. Anxiously, she
wondered whether Carlo would like it. It made her look
older, more mature, certainly. The figure in the mirror
was not Kate Melville, struggling artist from Wimbledon,

but a poised and beautiful Italian lady with the blonde hair and blue eyes that some Northern Italians occasionally possess.

A sudden bustle of excited femininity at the reception told her that Carlo had arrived. The young receptionist, with wide eyes and pink cheeks, came to call Kate, and she walked into the plant-filled reception area with beating heart, to find Carlo waiting for her. His splendid eyes took her in without any sign of surprise. He merely took her arm with a slight smile, and led her past the whispering, excited women to the door.

Kate was disappointed and irritated as she got into the Lancia. Why had he not commented on her hairstyle? Carlo put the car in gear.

'Is something the matter?' he asked calmly as he drove off.

'Nothing,' she said, tossing her new tresses resentfully. It had cost her the price of six months' supply of paints!

'I didn't want to say anything in front of all those stupid women, by the way,' he said gently, 'but you look beautiful, Caterina.'

'Do I?' she beamed.

'It's very pretty,' he assured her with a smile. 'You look very sexy now.'

'You mean I didn't before?'

'You were very sexy before,' he admitted, grinning. 'I should have said it makes you look very, *very* sexy. I'm taking you out into the country for some lunch, to a restaurant called Casa Botticelli. I thought you might like to try some Sicilian specialities?'

'That sounds lovely,' she said, settling back contentedly in the leather seat to enjoy the drive.

It was harsher countryside than that on Leparú, the

contrast between the rugged cliffs and the blue sea being most dramatic. Casa Botticelli was a charming old farm-house turned *ristorante*, set on the edge of an olive grove overlooking the sea. They took a table outside in the sun, on the terrace that gazed down at the blue water. As always, Carlo commanded instant attention without rais-ing a finger, and as she allowed him to order the meal, Kate was aware that several female heads were turned their way to admire him. And she was surprised to notice that several men were looking *her* way, too. A middle-aged man at the next table smiled at her, and she nodded coolly in return. It must be her new haircut, she decided, which was making her look more worldly.

It was a lovely day, a lovely spot, and once again she was facing Carlo Castelli across a table, fencing with those wonderful eyes. As they began their first course, a deli-cious spaghetti with little mussels, Kate asked Carlo about his computer empire.

He told her the story entertainingly and well, without either talking down to her or talking over her head. As she listened to him, Kate reflected on the depth of his per-sonality, the power and authority which he carried so lightly. He was a very rich man, and physically a very beautiful one, yet she had never detected the slightest sign of vanity in him. His tastes were exquisite, but never showy; his concepts were delightful, yet never extrava-gant. And even though, as he was telling her, he had worked his way to his present position by sheer brilliance and hard work, there was none of the arrogance about him which Kate had come to associate with self-made men. Carlo Castelli had risen from aristocratic poverty to a position of considerable prestige; he had shed the old-fashioned title of 'Prince', to which he was entitled by descent, as a meaningless bauble. And pride had never marked him. Not worldly pride, that is, the pride that comes of status and too much privilege; for in himself, as a superb male animal, Carlo was gloriously, triumphantly proud. He enjoyed his own supreme physical fitness, his dominating sexuality, with the same pleasure he took in driving his thoroughbred sports car. Kate knew instinctively that Carlo would be ruthless with himself, would drive himself to achieve the best in every field he attempted. She had never in her life considered the question of any man's sexual prowess, yet it was blindingly obvious that Carlo Castelli would be an unforgettable, unique lover. Because behind the simple physical act of love would lie the dedication, the pure power, of a master spirit.

She watched the light in his eyes, as it danced and glittered, and at the proud curve of his bold mouth—a mouth to set any woman dreaming. And suddenly it came to her—the reason why she had always been so shy, so awkward, in this man's presence. It was not because of his teasing, or because she was riled by his vast sex-appeal. No—for Carlo had always tried to put her at her ease, as he did with everyone he met, as though recognising that others would be threatened by so potent a figure and a personality as his.

It was because she loved him.

The realisation dropped through Kate's being like a stone dropped through clear water, changing everything she had assumed until that moment about herself, Carlo, the world. She had been falling in love with Carlo ever since that evening when he had first walked through her door and smiled into her eyes.

And at the same time, she realised with bitter force that she would never be able to tell him how she felt about him. He was a unique individual, the president of a vast financial corporation; while she was little more than a child to him, a plaything, who had tumbled accidentially into his life by the odd coincidence of an eccentric uncle's eccentric will. She sat staring at him, the knowledge of her own love swelling inside her, dominating every other thought, every feeling she had ever known. It was an emotion which seemed to fill her whole body, not so much a thrill as a deep ache, a kind of delicious bruise that had taken over her mind and heart completely.

This was why she had been put upon the earth, why she had struggled, why she had found herself in Wimbledon with a barely-begun career, why Roger had died—so that she could meet Carlo Castelli, and love him with all her being.

He looked up, suddenly aware that she was gazing at him with huge, brilliant eyes.

'Have I said something?' he smiled gently.

'What?' she asked in a whisper.

'You look strange, *cara*—have I said something to upset you? Don't you like your food?'

She blinked, emerging from her shell with an effort. A little colour touched her cheeks, but she smiled at him, and shook her head.

'I was dreaming,' she said softly. 'Yes, it *was* something you said—it just set me dreaming for a minute. I'm sorry, Carlo, please go on with what you were saying.'

He looked at her strangely, his dark brows lowered.

'What was it I said, Caterina?'

'It would be too difficult to explain,' she smiled. 'Now it's you who look strange—what is it?'

'You've changed,' he said slowly. 'Quite suddenly, over the last minute. I can't quite put my finger on it. You look different. You—you even talk differently.'

'Is it a change for the better?' she asked quietly, losing herself in the clear depths of his eyes.

'It's as though you've suddenly grown up,' he said seriously. 'Perhaps it's just the way they've cut your hair . . .'

'It must be,' she said calmly, and drank a little Frascati from her glass, feeling the cool, fruit-fresh white wine sliding down her throat. Carlo stared at her for a moment more, frowning. Then he shook some thought away. 'What would you like next?' he asked. 'There's some excellent veal—or you could try the roast pork.'

'I'm not really hungry,' said Kate with a smile.

'Nor am I,' he confessed. 'Let's just have the cassata, and then get back to Leparú for a swim.'

By early afternoon, they were back on *Coco*, and Carlo was steering the motor-launch through the colourful confusion of yachts and fishing boats to the harbour entrance. As they breasted the waves past the breakwater, and set course across the sparkling waves for the island, Kate was deep in thought.

She was under no illusions that her realisation at Casa Botticelli was going to—had already begun to—change her life. It was not that she herself was any different. She was still Kate Melville, shy and ignorant about the world; but her perception of that world would never be the same again. All her brave talk about her indifference to men had been simply a disguise for the overwhelming fact that she loved only one man. As she watched him turning the wheel with sure, safe hands, her heart yearned out to him with a pain that was almost too much to bear.

Yet what future could there be for her feelings about Carlo? It was inconceivable that he could return her feeling in any way. Carlo Castelli would have had dozens of beautiful women in his life. The richest, cleverest, most beautiful women in Italy would all have been available to him—how could he be interested in poor Kate? He had said that she was sexy—and that was the limit to which his interest would extend. If she let him, Carlo would take her, for a night's pleasure. Perhaps even for a week, until he saw the love in her eyes too clearly, and realised that the pleasure was over. Then he would simply walk away, and leave her with the pieces of her life. Parting from Carlo was a terrifying prospect in any case; but parting from him having once given him her body, having once held him in her arms to take his passion, would destroy her.

And what of Leparú itself? The beautiful island was a millstone around her neck. Could Carlo seriously intend to marry Vera in order to secure their rights to the island? The thought shot through her like a spear, making her gasp with pain. She could never stand by and watch Carlo go through the mockery of a marriage to Vera. Rather let Leparú be turned into a home for retired donkeys than that!

And what if—what if the dice fell the other way? What if Carlo chose to marry *her*—a brief, meaningless alliance to satisfy the shallow legal whim of a bizarre will? What would she say then? Again Kate winced. That would be a bitter irony, indeed! To have been married to Carlo, for a week—to be able to call herself Kate Castelli, in name but not in fact—it was too cruel to contemplate. She decided with sudden clarity that she would never concede to such an arrangement.

Would the best thing not be to flee—to run away, now, as far and as fast as she could, the way she had wanted to after that glorious night on the Thames?

'Oh, Uncle Roger,' she sighed into the salty breeze, 'if you only knew what you'd done to me!' She stared absently at the long, dark line of clouds that had appeared on the horizon behind them, trying to puzzle her way through the strange position she was in.

As they approached Leparú, Carlo turned to her.

'Let's not go straight back to the jetty,' he suggested. 'There are some beautiful beaches on the eastern side of the island—Roger and I discovered them once. You can only get to them by boat, because they're completely closed off by cliffs. It's very wild, but very beautiful. You'd like it.' He looked at her enquiringly. 'It seems a shame not to visit them, now that we've got *Coco*. Shall we go there?'

'It sounds lovely,' she nodded. 'Please let's go!'

He nodded, and swung the wheel, then accelerated past the long jetty, and began to steer the launch around the island.

Within a few minutes they were out of sight of the villa, and steering past the wild, rugged side of Leparú. Kate gazed up at the steep grey cliffs, gleaming in the brilliant sunlight, and reflected that Sicily was a place of contrasts. Like a passionate lover, it was alternately rough and gentle, kind and ruthless. About three miles past the villa and the long white beach, Carlo began to urge *Coco* inshore. Kate looked apprehensively at the jagged black rocks that protected the coast like savage sentinels. The normally blue water became an odd, disturbing green near them and the yeasty froth that the waves made over the volcanic rock was alarming.

'Are you sure it's safe?' she asked nervously.

'Nothing's absolutely safe as far as the sea's concerned,' he smiled. 'Not even in the placid Mediterranean. But I've done this before.' He steered the launch through a gap in the foaming reefs, and the powerful boat shuddered violently in the turbulent water. All the blue had suddenly vanished, and everywhere Kate looked, the sea was a livid cloudy green. The black teeth of the rocks seemed frighteningly close to *Coco*'s fibreglass hull, and the crash of the waves against them had become almost loud enough to drown out the comforting thud of the engines.

Only her utter trust in Carlo prevented her from giving way to panic as the boat thrust vigorously against the surging water, fighting a path through the reefs. Kate had a horrible feeling that any second a razor-sharp submerged reef was going to rip *Coco*'s bottom out; but within a few seconds Carlo had piloted the boat safely through the ugly place, and the white-and-green terror of the reefs was fading behind them. Carlo's eyes met hers with a grin. The danger had brought a light into his eyes that made her heart ache.

'Were you scared?'

'Not a bit,' she quavered, forcing a smile.

'*I* was,' he chuckled. 'I'm not as brave as you, obviously. Now look there—what do you think of that?' They were in a delightful little bay of calm blue water, encircled all around by the black teeth of the reef. The crescent-shaped beach ahead was golden-white, gleaming invitingly in the sun. It, too, was sealed off at either end by the rocks, and behind it the crumbling grey wall of the cliff rose upwards for two hundred feet. The gulls wheeled in the air above, greeting them joyfully. It was a savage and beautiful place, as wild as any scene that humans had ever set eyes on, yet tamed by a Mediterranean softness, bathed in blessed Mediterranean sunlight.

Carlo beached the launch carefully, sprang out, and moored it by its thick nylon rope to a great slap of basalt that lay at the water's edge. Kate took off her shoes, and lifting her dress modestly, waded ashore after him. The place was charming, a safe little enclave, utterly private, utterly secluded. She threw herself down on the hot sand, and thrust her fingers and toes into its welcoming warmth. Carlo arrived carrying their towels, and stood next to her, hands on hips, looking at the sea.

'It looks lovely, doesn't it?' he said. 'Let's go for a dip, and then lie in the sun.'

'I haven't brought a costume,' she wailed regretfully.

'That's not exactly a tragedy,' he smiled. 'There's no one here to see.'

'*You're* here,' she said firmly.

'Very well then, we'll go in in our underwear,' he said, 'like civilised people.'

Kate thought of what she had put on that morning, and her heart failed her.

'Male underwear is always a lot more suitable for swimming in than female underwear,' she said awkwardly. 'I'm not sure mine's quite appropriate.'

'Come on, little hedgehog,' he laughed, 'I promise you I'm quite tame.' He stripped off the clothes he was wearing, while Kate sat red-faced, staring pointedly in the opposite direction.

'Come on,' he growled, 'or I'll throw you in.'

Alarmed, she looked at him, and inspected his attire briefly. Once again she had forgotten the sheer magnificence of his body. The briefs he wore were almost indecent, and Kate stood up with an unhappy expression.

'Look the other way,' she commanded, as she slipped the light dress off.

'I'll be waiting for you in the water,' he laughed, and she watched his broad back departing, her heart sinking. The lacy bra and flowered pants she wore were alarmingly flimsy, but a quick examination reassured her that she was not exactly indecent. She tugged her bra a little tighter and followed Carlo's strong figure into the water.

It was delicious. The natural barrier reduced the waves to little more than light ripples, and the water was almost as calm as a swimming bath, and easily as clear. The sun had warmed the water unevenly, and alternating warm and cool current drifted across her body delightfully. She allowed herself to float, feeling the sun hot on her shoulders, and gazed up into the deep blue sky.

Carlo swam up to her with powerful strokes, and she smiled at him.

'I knew you'd like it,' he grinned. His handsome face was beaded with water, and Kate watched the muscles in his shoulders swelling rhythmically as he trod water.

'It's beautiful,' she said. 'Did you come here with Roger?'

He nodded. 'It was one of his favourite places on the island. There are some caves at the bottom of the cliff—we'll explore them later on, if you like.'

They drifted lazily in the blue water for half an hour. Kate was enchanted with the bay. Through the clear depths she could see shells on the sandy bottom, starfish, and pink and white stones. She half expected to see a treasure chest lying half open, its gorgeous contents spilling out into the calm, ultramarine water.

At length they waded ashore. Kate had almost forgotten the flimsiness of her attire, until she saw Carlo's expression. She looked down in dismay. The water had reduced her pants and bra to a stage of such clinging transparency that she was little better than naked! Hastily she wrapped her towel around her torso, her face feeling hot. Carlo shook his head ruefully.

'My poor hedgehog! Why are you ashamed of your body? It's so beautiful. It was made to be seen and admired, not to be hidden away.'

She glared at him. 'It wasn't made to be looked at in the way *you* were looking at it,' she said crossly.

Carlo burst out laughing, the muscles of his chest and stomach pulsing with merriment. 'Come on,' he said, 'let's go and explore those caves.'

She walked with him to the bottom of the cliff, trying to keep her eyes off his near-naked figure. Somehow he seemed to fit perfectly into this savagely beautiful setting, his own physical perfection matching the natural beauty of the bay. The dark blue briefs he wore hugged his body disturbingly closely, and Kate found him a fascinating, heart-stopping figure. The cave before them was over-hung by a shelf of rock, and although its entrance was wide, it seemed to extend quite a long way into the cliff.

The sand on the bottom of the cave was cool under Kate's bare feet, and the back of the long rock chamber was dark.

'Nothing—*lives* here, does it?' she enquired apprehensively.

'You mean like lions and tigers,' he suggested rather drily. 'No. These caves were worn out by the sea, millions of years ago—they're not inhabited by anything.'

Kate glanced back thoughtfully at the blue water.

'The sea doesn't come up as far as this, does it?'

'Not in the normal course. I suppose it might do in very

bad weather—but it's quite safe now.'

The interior of the cave was pleasantly cool and dark after the hot afternoon sun, and she settled down in the sand, running it through her fists. Carlo smiled down at her.

'You're going to have to sacrifice your towel,' he said gently.

'What?'

'For the common good. I can't sit next to you because my pants are wet. But if you lay your towel down, we can both sit in peace.'

Unhappily, Kate unwound her towel, thinking that it was probably too dark in the cave to see much anyway. She spread it out, and Carlo sat down next to her, his hard, warm arm brushing her naked side. She shivered, and clasped her arms tightly around her drawn-up knees.

'Are you still frightened of me?' he asked gently.

'I never was frightened of you,' she said defiantly, but a tremor in her voice betrayed her.

'What's the matter?' he asked in concern. 'You're shaking, *cara*. Are you cold?'

'A little,' she said quietly, unable to stop her body's instinctive reaction to his proximity.

Carlo's deep voice was worried. 'I hope you haven't got a chill. It's not impossible, even in the middle of summer. Perhaps we'd better get back to the villa.'

'No—it's all right, really.' She smiled at him in the bluish light of the cavern. 'It's not a chill. Maybe someone walked over my grave again.'

'Maybe it's me,' he said softly.

'Maybe it is,' she whispered. His arm came around her trembling shoulders, and he pushed her gently on to her back.

'No, Carlo—please—'

'Shh!' He leaned over her. 'Even hedgehogs have to uncurl sometimes. Do you think I'm going to hurt you?'

'No, but—'

'Don't be so tense.' He brushed the soft hair away from her forehead, his mouth smiling down at her calmly. 'I've been wanting to tell you all day how lovely you look, Caterina. It's been weeks since we kissed—I've been missing it.'

'What are Vera's lips like?' she asked nervously. His touch on her face was maddeningly gentle, and she could feel her stomach fluttering rapidly.

'Don't be silly,' he said.

'Vera's beautiful.'

'Who wants to talk about Vera?' he asked. His lips brushed her cheek, and she felt his warm breath stir in her hair. She could not stop a little moan breaking from her.

'You were rubbing sin-cream into her. I mean sun-cream.'

'Sin-cream sounds better,' he said, his laughter soft and low. 'What of it? I couldn't very well leave her to roast, could I?'

'Do you like her?' Kate asked shakily.

'Vera? Of course I like her.'

'No,' she said, 'I mean—you know, in *that* way.'

'Ah,' he smiled, 'in *that* way. Sure, Vera's a bit of hot stuff.'

'Carlo!' He grinned at her wickedly, his eyes shining in the dim light from the entrance of the cave.

'Anyway, let's not talk about Vera,' he said. 'I want to get to the bottom of this shivering of yours. I wonder if there's any way I can stop it?'

She tried to resist the sweet coercion of his mouth, turning her head away.

'Don't!' she pleaded.

'Are you still convinced that you are made of ice, *cara*?'

'No,' she breathed. 'I know all too well that I'm only flesh, Carlo.'

'And what flesh!' he smiled. 'You're so beautiful, Caterina—you make any other woman look drab next to you.'

'Carlo,' she begged, 'let's get back into the boat and go back to the villa.' She stared up into his face, knowing that if he touched her again, she would be helpless. Her body was yearning for him, a hollow ache that only he could satisfy. And the consciousness that his desire matched hers was making her head swim. Yet she knew that he would only want her until his need was spent, while she—she would want him for ever.

'Don't you trust me?' he asked softly.

'It's not that,' she whispered. 'I don't trust myself. Please let's go.'

'No,' he said, his voice a tender growl. 'I want you.'

CHAPTER EIGHT

KATE had expected his lips to be demanding and rough, like the lips of other men who had tried to kiss her; yet his gentleness took her breath away. It was a kiss designed to give pleasure, not only to take it. It was impossible to fight against so wonderfully tender a caress—there was nothing to resist.

'There,' he purred, 'was that so bad?'

'It was beautiful, Carlo, but I still think—' His mouth silenced hers with another soft meeting.

'This is the first kiss I've ever taken from you, *cara*, which you haven't resisted,' he smiled. 'Now kiss me back.'

'No,' she gasped. 'Don't make me lose my head!'

'Hedgehog,' he growled. His lips met hers fiercely this time, forcing her mouth open, demanding a response. Kate tried to clear her mind, tried to ignore the throbbing need that was welling up in her. She shut her eyes.

'Kiss me back,' he commanded. She shook her head, her breath coming light and fast. 'Very well,' he said quietly, 'I'll make you kiss me.'

Kate braced herself for the onslaught, but none came. Instead, his lips brushed her face with wicked, tantalising skill, leaving a little trail of fire from throat to chin, touching her ears and temples with the lightness of a butterfly's wing. Wherever his lips met her tender skin, a new awareness seemed to flicker into life, and her arms were beginning to creep across his naked back. Desire was running through her in a long flame, the way a brush-fire possesses dry grass, beginning to dominate her entire being with its vivid, irresistible heat. She drew her face away, her heart pounding in her ears, and tried to sit up, brushing her hair away from her face with a trembling hand.

She heard Carlo's purring laughter, and then his arms reached for her, pulling her against him with ruthless power. His chest was warm, and Kate could feel the potency of the muscles under his velvety skin as he pressed her to him. She buried her face in the warmth of his neck, breathing the intoxicating smell of his skin into her nostrils. She could taste the sea-salt on his skin, and her arms clasped his powerful, infinitely secure shoulders as helplessly as a child.

'Don't do this to me,' she whispered against his neck. 'It's not fair!'

'What makes you resist?' he asked with bone-melting gentleness, raising her head with tender power from his shoulder.

She gazed, almost hypnotised, into the dark magnificence of his face.

'Can't you understand? Don't you know how I feel about you, Carlo?'

'Tell me,' he invited, an amused glint in the deep green emeralds of his eyes.

She shook her head helplessly. 'I don't mean physically,' she said softly.

'What makes you think I'm only interested in your physique?' he smiled, pushing her down on to the soft towel again, and leaning over her with a deeply amused, calm smile. 'Tell me everything, *cara* . . .' With each kiss, he had made Kate's senses swim a little more. Now,

Carlo's mouth was unambiguously desirous, and her pulses leaped.

'You're so much stronger than I am,' she gasped. 'I can't stop you from doing what you want to, you know that! Why won't you respect my wishes?'

'You don't even know your own wishes, Caterina mine,' he said against her ear. 'Let me help you make your mind up.'

'You could force me, Carlo,' she said bitterly. 'We both know that. But I'm not going to co-operate.'

'Aren't you?' She lay completely still, determined not to respond to his kisses again. 'My little cold sea-nymph,' he mocked. He took her lower lip in his teeth, as he had done once before, and bit sharply. Her little yelp echoed in the blue darkness of the cave, and his chuckle was wicked. His arms slid underneath her, crushing her against him with iron force, pressing their near-naked bodies together, and the searing flame of his lips ran across her mouth, from corner to corner, in an expert, dizzying caress, that was too wicked to be borne tamely. She wrestled against him madly, thrusting her own soft body against his hard power, but he was like supple steel, and the sure strength of his muscles clamped against her resistance. His mouth met hers with no veiling of mockery now. His body was an authority that could no longer be disobeyed, his mouth a tyrant that thrust through her defences and plundered the sweetness of her mouth without mercy.

Her arms clasped his neck without thought as her own passion, for too long held in check, rose to meet his. They were too scantily clad for his desire to be concealed from her in any way. Kate shuddered voluptuously against the hard heat of his body, all pretence at indifference evaporating. In the consuming fire of his kiss, against the naked power of his body, she was becoming a woman.

He drew back, and rolled slightly away from her, his own breathing shallow and rapid. The wonderful smile that curved his lips thrilled Kate.

'The Sicilian sun has put some warmth in your heart after all, *cara*.'

'Perhaps it was never cold,' she said unevenly, trying to match his smile. His eyes dropped to her body with deliberate, unselfconscious admiration.

'Your skin is the colour of cream,' he purred gently, tracing a finger across her flinching stomach. 'After a few days in the sun, it will be the colour of wild honey. Caterina—I want to talk to you.' His fingers, almost unconsciously, were at the catch of her bra, between her breasts. She laid her own fingers on his gently.

'You can talk to me as I am,' she said shakily. She had meant to stop him, but somehow her hand was merely guiding his now, and the clasp opened, letting her bra slip gently away to either side. The expression in Carlo's eyes melted her very soul, and she gasped aloud as he stroked the rounded contours of her naked breasts with intimate, stunning, gentleness.

'Caterina.' His voice was a sigh. 'You're so beautiful, my dear . . .' His fingers brushed the aching tips of her breasts, and then she was in his arms, holding him desperately.

'Carlo—'

'I must say something to you, *cara*,' he murmured into her ear. 'About Leparú—and your Uncle Roger—and you and me —'

Suddenly there was an icy buffet of wind in the cave. Carlo's eyes widened, holding hers for a moment. In the silence, Kate could hear a dull booming echoing down the mouth of the cave. It had become cold, too, and unless she was mistaken, a good deal darker. He whispered an expletive under his breath, his face serious.

'Carlo, what is it?'

'Bring your towel,' he said, turning and striding to the entrance of the cave. Kate followed him, frightened, feeling the cold wet air blowing into the cave now, utterly unlike the warm air of half an hour earlier.

A terrible change had come over the bay. The sky had disappeared into a maelstrom of black, swirling cloud, and a high wind was whipping the sand off the beach like shrapnel. And the sea! Where a calm blue pool had been before was now a boiling mass of white and green waves. The protective crescent of rocks had disappeared under the yeasty torrent of the incoming sea. Kate clutched Carlo's arm desperately.

'What is it?' she repeated, her heart pounding.

His face was grim, his eyes terrible.

'It's a summer gale,' he grated. 'God, I've been a fool! I didn't think to listen for a gale warning—we were going such a short distance!' Suddenly Kate remembered the long line of ominous clouds that she had noticed on the journey back from Catania, and cursed herself for not having registered its meaning better, not having told Carlo. A sudden crack above the roar of the coming storm drew their attention to the launch. The wild sea had lifted it off the beach, and was now slamming it with horrible force against the basalt slab.

'God! I've got to try and cut *Coco* loose!'

'No—Carlo!' She tried to pull him back, but he thrust her into the entrance of the cave and raced across the whirling sand towards the boat. She watched in terror as he struggled with the mooring rope, waist-deep in the swirling water. The blackness of the sky was suddenly split with a livid flash of lightning, followed almost at once by a crash of thunder. Kate screamed, and at the same time Carlo lost his footing in the wild, evil water.

She stared desperately through the blowing sand, but there was no sign of him. With a flash of realisation that life would not be worth living if he were dead, she ran down to the water's edge, calling his name. The sea was smashing up the beach with terrible hammer-blows, and as she searched for a trace of Carlo in the increasingly savage water, the motor launch was lifted again, as if on the back of some vast, rearing sea-monster, and dashed on to the rock. With a splintering sound, the fibreglass hull was rent open. The sea snatched it up again, and again the boat careered into the rocks, splitting further.

Carlo's head suddenly appeared through the yellow whirlpool of the waves. Kate called to him again, the rising wind snatching the words from her mouth, and saw him swimming with powerful strokes against the riptide that was dragging him remorselessly towards the jagged black gallows of the rocks.

Again the sky flashed blue-white, and the thunder steamrollered across the bay. Taking advantage of a pause in the huge suck and surge of the waves, Carlo swam desperately towards the shore. He was almost within arm's length of her, and she could see the muscles straining across his shoulders, when the sea dragged him back with monstrous playfulness, and within a second he was lost in the waves again.

Panic-stricken, she pulled the hair out of her eyes, searching for something to throw to him. The wind was increasing by the minute, and the sea was getting visibly higher. Near-naked as she was, the spray and sand were lashing her cruelly. With another horrible splintering crash, the launch was battered on to the rocks again. The mooring rope! It had broken free of the boat's hull, and was floating at the water's edge, one end still tied to the basalt slab that was now half submerged. Frantically, Kate struggled with the knots, fear and cold making her fingers clumsy. After maddening moments, it came free, and she raced with her prize to the foaming edge of the waves, looking for Carlo. There was no sign of him for an agonising minute, and then she caught a glimpse of his brown skin appearing between the white shoulders of the breakers, mercifully close to her. She shouted to him above the howl of the gale, and hurled the rope to him. It fell short. Cursing despairingly, she dragged it back, and cast it out again, and this time Carlo caught it, slipped a little, held on.

Bracing her legs against the near-impossible strain, Kate hauled with every ounce of strength against the murderous pull of the sea.

A lucky breaker crashed on to the shore, throwing Carlo forward. In the pause, she ran backwards and pulled again. Suddenly he was in shallow water again, and staggering forward exhausted. She met him knee-deep in the foam, seizing both his hands in her own, and dragged him back on to the beach. They fell together on the cold sand, the wind lashing at them as they held each other with desperate strength.

Kate found she was sobbing. Her fingers were locked in the salty cold tangle of his hair, and his own arms were tight around her waist. With tightly-shut eyes, she breathed an inarticulate prayer of thankfulness. The sea crashing over their legs warned them that their position was by no means safe, and Carlo hauled himself to his feet, pulling her up. Her vision blurred with tears, she gazed into the grey-green depths of his eyes, catching the glint of his tired grin.

'I owe you something,' he called into the teeth of the wind. 'Let's get back to the cave!' He pulled her after him towards the base of the cliff. The sea had raced halfway up the beach by now. And with another mighty crash, the rain came, a pelting fury that knocked the breath out of Kate's lungs. Carlo paused to snatch their clothes out of the sea's grasp, wet and filled with sand, then ran with her to the mouth of the cave.

In the shelter of the rock overhang, she fell into his arms, her own strength now utterly gone.

'Oh, Carlo,' she sobbed, 'thank God you're safe—I thought I'd lost you!'

'I'm safe,' he smiled, hugging her tenderly, 'thanks to you, *cara*—my little heroine.' For the first time she noticed the thin red stain on her own arms, and then looked anxiously at his side.

'You're hurt!' she gasped, stooping to examine the wound.

'It's nothing,' he assured her. 'Put your dress on, Caterina—I know it's cold, but it'll help to protect you.' But he winced as he held the sodden dress out to her, and Kate examined the cut worriedly. He had been dashed against the razor-edge of a submerged rock, and the long, ugly gash beneath his ribs was welling bright hot blood across his cold skin. She bit her lip—the cut was unpleasantly deep, and she was horrified to see that the torn edge of the wound was bruised and livid.

'That must hurt terribly,' she said, looking up at him. His face was a pearly white, and the strain around his intense eyes told her that he was suffering. Quickly, she tore a long strip from the bottom of her skirt, and bound it as best she could around his ribs, trying to stem the oozing blood that continued to flow.

A shattering sound above the roar of the storm made them both turn to look down the beach. The launch had burst open like a mistreated child's toy, and even as they watched, the wild sea ripped the stern away and sucked it into the maelstrom.

'Well,' Carlo sighed bitterly, staring at the wreckage, 'that's the end of *Coco*.' He turned to her, his eyes dark. 'I'm sorry, *cara*—this is all my fault. I can't think how I was so stupid as to bring you here without checking the weather.'

'I wanted to come,' she said, smiling uncertainly. 'And it's my fault, too—I noticed the clouds coming up behind us, but I didn't think to warn you.'

'Caterina,' he said, taking her shoulders in his hands, and looking into her eyes, 'I'm afraid our position is serious.'

'Why?' she asked anxiously. 'Can't we just shelter in the cave until it's over?'

He shook his head gravely, and turned her to face the sea. The gale was blowing full force now, and the sea was hurling itself three-quarters of the way up the little crescent of beach.

'The sea will be here in a very few minutes,' he said gently. Kate's heart sank. 'In one quarter of an hour—maybe less—this cave will be submerged.'

She looked at him fear clutching at her throat for a second. 'You mean—we're going to die here?'

'If we stay here, we'll drown,' he nodded, his eyes calm on her face. Suddenly she felt a great calm surge through her, too, and she smiled up at him.

'Then I'm glad I'm with you,' she said simply.

'And I'm glad I'm with you,' he smiled. 'But we're not going to drown if I can help it. There is one way out—up the cliff.'

She stared at him in horror. 'But—it's practically vertical!' she gasped.

'I know,' he nodded. 'But it's our only chance. I've got the rope, for what it's worth. And I noticed what looks like an easy way up.'

'Easy?' she queried, and he grinned ruefully.

'At least not so impossible,' he admitted, and then looked at her seriously. 'It's either that, *cara*, or drown here like rats. We'll try and scale the cliff, and then find our way back to the villa. Will you try?'

She nodded silently, trusting him completely. As he pulled his pants and shirt gingerly over himself, she saw his eyes flicker to their feet. They were both barefoot—the sea had taken their sandals. She realised suddenly that his confident expression was merely a mask, designed to reassure her, and felt her love for him welling up inside her, an unbearably sweet and poignant load of passion for him. It suddenly occurred to her that they might both die in the next few minutes without her ever having told him how she felt about him. She took his hand quickly.

'Carlo—'

'Tell me later, sweetheart,' he interrupted. 'Put your dress on now—we haven't got more than a few minutes. When the Mediterranean gets angry, its temper runs very short indeed. Quickly!'

She tugged the cold, wet dress on. She had torn most of the bottom off to bandage his side, and it barely covered her thighs now—but it was better than nothing.

'I'm ready,' she told him.

He nodded briskly. 'Good—let's go.' He grasped her hand, and led her out into the raging storm.

The wind smashed against them like a giant fist, and the rain battered at them like a flail of ropes' ends. Kate had never experienced such naked power. It was as if the beautiful blue bay had never existed at all—as if it had been some sorcerer's mirage to lure them to this terrible violence.

Carlo dragged her along the beach. She glanced back for a second; all trace of the launch had vanished, though she thought she caught a swirl of something white being tossed in the breakers. But the sea was nearly at the cliff's edge, and beginning to thrust into the cave they had just left. At a crumbling ledge in the cliff, Carlo stopped. He did not bother trying to make himself heard above the appalling noise of the tempest, merely pointed at the ledge, waited for her nod, then hoisted her up. She scrambled to retain her foothold in the sharp, splintering rock as he clambered up beside her. The wind ripped at them angrily. With dismay, she saw that the scarlet stain at the side of his shirt was spreading.

Ignoring it, he pointed to another ledge higher up. Kate's heart failed her—it seemed impossibly far away, but he was already stooping to lift her up.

She grasped at the naked rock, feeling her fingertips scrape on the roughness of it, and slithered her way desperately upwards, trying to blot out the pain of her scraped knees and shins. For a horrible moment she was falling backwards, then he was beside her, one steely arm holding her forward against the cliff-face. She met his eyes, trying to seize the strength he was so obviously projecting out to her. Her lungs were heaving, and her heart pierced with cramps, but he was already showing her the long, narrow ledge that led steadily upwards to the next crumbling platform.

Exhausted, she scrambled upwards, trying not to lean back by so much as a fraction of an inch. The wind clawed at her, as though trying to hurl her down into the raging sea below, but once again he was close behind her, his sure strength ramming her back against the rock. At the next ledge they paused, their chests heaving. She glanced down at the sea, and her spirits lifted at how far they had already come. But when she looked upwards into the beating rain, despair swamped her again. It was too far! Already her muscles were aching, and she had scraped her breasts painfully against the unyielding stone.

Sensing her despair, Carlo took her arm and shook it angrily. He put his mouth against her ear, and shouted, 'Courage! Wait here—I'll pull you up!' She nodded weakly. He looped the end of the boat's mooring-rope around her waist, and fastened it expertly. Then, with a grim smile, he reached upwards and hauled himself with sheer animal force on to the next tiny ledge, the end of the rope clenched in his teeth.

Kate watched him climb, the brutal rain pelting into her upturned face, marvelling at his courage and power. At the top of the little step he turned carefully, so that his back was against the cliff, and shouted down to her. His words were snatched away by the gale, but she understood his meaning and braced herself. As he hauled steadily at the rope, it cut cruelly into her ribs, making her gasp with pain—but she was lifting! She scrabbled at the rock with her feet, thrusting herself upwards, and after a stomach-turning few seconds, she was in his arms, and he was pulling her on to the ledge next to him.

Tears of pain and fear had streaked her cheeks, mingling with the rain and the sea-spray. Carlo brushed them away with a brief smile, hugging her wordlessly, as the wind wrenched at their bodies.

'I love you!' she screamed against the wind, but he did not hear. He pointed at the overhang above, not more than a scramble away, then thrust her onwards. Her ankle twisted agonisingly as she pushed herself on to the harsh platform of rock, and lay there, shaking and exhausted. He clambered up next to her, the side of his shirt soaked red by now, and rolled her on to her back, lifting her, so that she could see upwards. There was barely twenty yards to go, and new hope fired her. He lifted her, and she pointed to her ankle, wincing. He nodded, slipping his arm around her shoulders, and urged her onwards to the next goal.

It seemed an eternity later that they were facing the last ledge before the top. Kate looked up, her stomach heaving. The ledge was just out of reach, and her aching shoulders could barely support the weight of her upraised arms. Carlo knelt, clasping her around her hips, and heaved her up. She grasped at the rock wildly, as he placed her feet on his shoulders, and pushed her up. Suddenly, to her horror, the crumbling rock gave way, and she slithered back in a landslide of stones and rubble, the top of the cliff so tantalisingly close. She tottered on Carlo's iron shoulders for a second, then collapsed on to him with a shriek.

She was certain that they were falling, falling, down to the hungry sea below, but he had grasped her waist and was holding her with the strength born of desperation, as she swayed out over the void. Then, slowly, surely, he drew her back, and without hesitation, lifted her up to the ledge once more. This time the rock she seized held firm, and she dragged herself painfully over the lip of the cliff, to collapse on to the bracken at the top, as the wind howled resentfully over her. In a minute Carlo had clawed his way after her, and was lying beside her, his broad chest heaving in the lashing rain. Kate shut her eyes, too numb to do more than thank God.

Another frightful crash of thunder stirred her. Carlo was on his knees next to her, his beautiful face drawn and grey. Yet there was still a smile on the bold mouth, and his tawny eyes were alight. He pulled her carefully to her feet. She gasped as the pain darted through her sprained ankle, and he led her through the pouring rain to a little clump of twisted olive trees, whose tangled branches were lashing in the wind.

In the partial shelter, she clung to him, suddenly conscious of a thousand pains that she had been too wrought up to notice before—the stinging lacerations on her hands and bare feet, the bruises across her ribs and hips. He stroked her wet hair gently, his arm comfortingly about her shoulders. The sea below bore not the slightest resemblance to the calm blue Mediterranean she had bathed in less than two hours earlier. Cold and shivering, she stared with glazed eyes at the raging waves for a few moments. Had they remained in that cave—had they not succeeded in their terrible climb—they would now both be cold and dead, tossed in the vast claws of that monster below. The thought brought on a fit of shuddering sobs.

She knew that only Carlo could possibly have brought them through. Only his physical strength and fitness, his indomitable will, could have carried them both up that sheer cliffside in the midst of a gale.

He tilted her head up with a hand under her chin, and looked urgently into her eyes.

'Can you walk?' She nodded uncertainly, trying to draw strength from his face. 'We can't stay here,' he called into her ear. 'Nobody knows where we are—even the boat's gone. If they find the wreckage, they'll think we've sunk.' She nodded her understanding miserably, leaning against his hard strength. 'It's getting late, too,' he continued. 'It's going to be night soon, and this storm will be raging for hours yet. I don't like the way you're shivering—I want to get you back to the villa. Understand?'

Kate squeezed his hand, and bent wearily to look at the cut in his side. Under her inadequate makeshift bandage, the gash had begun to clot at last; but it was still seeping blood, and a dark bruise had spread across his ribs under the golden skin. Carlo shook her attentions away impatiently, shaking his head. 'I'll be fine,' he called. 'By my estimate, it's about two miles to the villa. Maybe three—not more.' The lightning speared down again, and another burst of thunder brought a renewed onslaught of rain and wind. 'Can you walk that far?' he asked, seeking her eyes seriously.

'I'll try,' she said, trying to smile.

'*Brava!* Put your arm over my shoulder.' Supporting her against his own good side, he led her down from the edge of the cliff, into the thicket of thrashing olive trees.

She had been unaware until now of her exhaustion, and every time she put her injured foot down, a frightening pain shot through her ankle. Within a few paces she was giddy with pain and tiredness, and she sagged against him. The thunder roared savage mockery overhead, and the wind thrust her to her knees. Carlo hauled her up again, and urged her on. The three miles ahead seemed as impossible to Kate as three thousand. The elemental fury of the weather, combined with her assorted pains and fears, seemed about to crush her. They staggered forward into the teeth of the wind for five minutes, and then she could move no further. She leaned against him, the tears spilling helplessly out of her eyes.

'I'm sorry,' she gasped.

He shook his head, smiling tenderly at her. 'Rest,' he called, and lowered her on to the ground. She closed her eyes, feeling the sleep of surrender rising up to claim her. It seemed only seconds later that he was pulling her to her feet again, and slipping his arm around her neck to support her. They walked slowly on, through a landscape that was torn apart with rain and wind, battered with thunder. The branches of trees whipped in the high wind, and it was often impossible to see more than a few yards ahead. She trusted to Carlo to find the right way. The world all around was a roaring wilderness that was implacably, utterly hostile to them. From the gentle piece of paradise it had been, Leparú had become a purgatory.

Another agonising stretch later, Kate was down again. She lay in Carlo's arms, feeling that her strength had finally given way.

'I'm sorry,' she whispered, her eyelids flickering closed.

'It doesn't matter,' he said against her cheek as he lifted her up. 'You sleep now—I'll carry you for a little while.'

'No,' she gasped, struggling free, 'your side!' With desperate strength she walked on, leaning on Carlo's arm.

It was becoming much darker now; the night was drawing in, and it dawned on Kate that it might be very serious to be caught in the gale all night. She was under no delusions that she herself was exhausted, and slightly shocked; and the bleeding in Carlo's side had still not

stopped. Unless it was strapped up or stitched soon, he
would be in danger of severe blood-loss, and perhaps even
an infection brought on by his wet, dirty clothes.

Through the howling of the gale, she caught his shout.
She followed his pointing finger, trying to see through the
sheets of rain. A path! They made their way towards it
slowly, and at last Kate's spirits began to rise. The pain in
her ankle was a vast ache, but a steady numbness was
taking over her senses. She stumbled helplessly on the wet
gravel, and Carlo caught her up short. He turned her in
his arms and looked into her face in concern. She smiled
stiffly. His own face was pale and drawn, and with his
magnificent eyes and tight mouth, he looked to her like
some marble Crusader, arisen from his tomb.

The thought that he might die terrified her, and she
fought against the overwhelming numbness, driving herself forward, so as not to be a burden on him.

They stumbled on into the storm, and despite her good
intentions she was soon dragging on his shoulder, the pain
in her ankle almost too much to bear.

There was something familiar about the trees they were
passing under. Through the curtain on the rain, she stared
blindly at the little wood, the outcrop of rock. Yes—it was
the ancient altar, the place where she had found the clay
lamp with the satyr on it. Relief swept through her. She
saw Carlo's smile through the gathering darkness, and a
little flicker of new energy drove her on. Soon they were in
the lemon grove, and the lights of the villa were twinkling
ahead of them. And someone was hurrying towards them
with a hurricane lamp and an umbrella. An umbrella!
Kate was laughing weakly as Rosario took her other arm,
and guided them down to the house.

CHAPTER NINE

Sara's round face was worried as she carried the steaming mugs of cocoa over to them. They were in the kitchen of the villa, beside the roaring fire that Rosario had lit in the vast grate.

'*Terribile!*' she said, gesturing to the windows where the storm was battering. Kate sipped at the steaming drink, infinitely grateful for its reviving warmth. A large pot of some savoury stew was on its way.

'We were so afraid that you'd drowned,' said Vera, looking at them with huge eyes. 'Dear God, you look as though you've been in a battle!'

'We'll get cleaned up in a minute,' said Carlo. He turned his pale, exhausted face to Rosario. 'Have you been through to the coastguards?' he asked.

Rosario shook his head.

'The gale blew down the radio-telephone mast in the first few minutes, *padrone*. I have never seen anything like this before. We've been marooned here—we were unable even to call out a search party for you and the Signorina Caterina.'

'We'll get it fixed again when the storm's blown over,' Carlo answered, gulping at his cocoa.

Sara gently lifted the blanket she had wrapped around him, and raised his shirt to examine the wound under his ribs. She caught her breath, her eyes widening in horror. Vera gasped.

'You're cut!' she exclaimed, her own face becoming pale. 'How did you do that?'

'Trying to cut the launch loose,' he grimaced, touching the inflamed skin gingerly. 'I thought it would have a better chance of surviving if it was free of the rocks.'

Rosario shook his head in wonder: 'How you climbed the cliff is a mystery, *padrone*. But like that—it's a miracle you are both alive!'

The thunder rumbled overhead as if to underline his words. Sara clucked angrily, her dark eyes grief-stricken as she peered at the wound

'*Ospedale*,' she said, pointing to the cut, and making sewing motions with her hand. '*Punti—presto, presto!*'

'Is there a first-aid kit in the house?' Kate asked. Rosario spoke to his wife in rapid dialect, and she nodded, answering him eagerly. He disappeared, and came back a moment later carrying a large white box with a red cross on it.

Kate hobbled over and inspected the contents. 'Do you know anything about first-aid?' she asked Vera anxiously.

Vera shook her head hastily. 'I'm no good at that sort of thing at all,' she said in a miserable voice. 'I can't bear the sight of blood!'

Carlo drank off the rest of his cocoa, and smiled rather painfully at Kate. 'You'd better attend to me yourself, my dear Caterina.'

Kate studied his face, feeling her own exhaustion giving way to anxiety. He was deathly white, and dark bruises had appeared under the tawny eyes that still glowed with fierce energy. She stooped, wincing at the pain in her ankle, and looked at the gash across his side. The wound was ugly, and the whole area seemed to be angry and swollen. Her heart tripped unpleasantly. The storm was still raging, and there was no chance of getting to a hospital within hours—perhaps days. The cut had been savagely deep, and in the hours since those dreadful moments at the little bay, it had never been clean. With the terrible exertions he had undergone, the torn muscles had been strained and overworked to a serious degree. The skin around the wound was hot. She touched his forehead quickly—it was burning.

He looked at her with an ironic smile.

'Will I live?' he asked drily.

Kate tried to stop her anxiety from showing, and smiled tiredly at him.

'You just might,' she said lightly. 'Let's have some of that stew quickly, and then I'll try and clean the cut a little.'

'Please count me out,' said Vera anxiously, then smiled uncertainly. 'I hate to see anything like that,' she said unhappily, 'it makes me faint.'

'I'll go and close all the shutters,' said Rosario, and Sara began to serve up the stew.

After they had eaten a little, Rosario helped Kate support Carlo to his bedroom, and left her there with the first-aid box and a ewer of boiling water. Carlo lay back on the pillows, watching her with an amused expression in his grey-green eyes as she tore cottonwool into little swabs.

'Have you done any nursing before?' he drawled. 'I hope I'm not your first patient.' The gale tore at the house with huge hands, pounding on the doors and shutters, and Kate shivered.

'You saved my life to-day,' she said quietly, as she dipped one of her swabs in the hot water and began to dab at the encrusted blood.

Carlo smiled at her. 'And you saved mine. If you hadn't thrown that rope to me, I'd have been halfway to Africa by now—under the water.' She shuddered at the thought, and dabbed at the edges of the wound as gently as she could. The beautiful male body in front of her had lost its golden tint. It was now the colour of electrum, and the powerful muscles lay quiet, as though graven out of some precious stone. The area around the long gash was a dark red, and it seemed to Kate that she could see the sinister stain spreading as she looked. Carlo watched her with enigmatic eyes.

'Are you going to stitch it?' he asked.

She shook her head. 'I don't think I could bear to,' she said. 'I just want to get as much dirt and dried blood out of it as possible.' She bit her lip as she sponged the wound, well aware of how dreadfully painful it must be for him. He did not flinch, but at one point his eyelids dropped over his eyes, and when he opened them again, they had become dark.

'Carlo—' she said hesitantly. 'I think—I think there's an infection setting in.'

'*Brava,*' he said with soft irony. He was burning hot, and a light sheen had appeared across his face and chest.

'We've got to get you to a hospital,' she said miserably. 'How long will the storm last?'

He shook his head. 'I'm not a weather prophet,' he said drily. The rain rattled on the shutter like grapeshot, and he turned his eyes to her. 'When the storm dies down, you'll have to get the radio mast back up somehow. Rosario will do it if you help him. Understand?' She nodded, twisting her hands. 'Then you'll have to call the coastguards. There is another boat on Leparú, but it's a yacht. You couldn't possibly sail it in this weather, even if you knew how to.'

She nodded again, and began to make a bandage to lay over the wound. Now more than ever, Carlo was like the marble image of some Crusader. Pallor had revealed the nobility of his features, and the fine, pale face that watched her with an ironic quirk of the eye-brow was a true prince's. Only his eyes were vivid, glittering with a cold, tawny light. The contrast between the icy cold of his face and the heat of the wound terrified her.

'There's morphia in the box,' she told him. 'Though I don't know how good I'd be at giving an injection.'

'No, thank you,' he said. 'Is there any aspirin?'

'There's paracetamol,' she said, tipping three of the white tablets into her hand, and pouring him a glass of water. He drank, his hands unsteady on the glass, then lay back. Despite the cold of his skin, he was still sweating. The howl of the gale rose and fell outside. Gingerly Kate laid the bandage over the cut under his ribs. With its redness invisible, he looked less frightening to her. His head settled back on the pillows as she pulled the covers carefully over him. He smiled at her slightly, closing his eyes. Within a few seconds, his breathing had become regular and shallow. At last Kate gave way to the luxury of a huge yawn, and sank down at the bottom of the bed, her exhaustion finally claiming her.

Vera's touch awoke her. The wind was still roaring over the house, and it was cold. She had fallen asleep with her arms and head on the foot of Carlo's bed. He was sleeping restlessly.

'Don't you want to get some sleep?' asked Vera, her pretty face concerned. 'I'll stay with Carlo, if you like.'

Kate rose stiffly, feeling each bruise in her body.

'What time is it?' she asked.

'Four o'clock in the morning,' said Vera. 'The gale's still blowing.' She looked at Carlo. 'Is he—going to die?'

'Not if I can help it,' said Kate grimly. 'Do you think I could have some coffee?'

'Sure.' Vera disappeared, and Kate looked down at Carlo's sleeping face. It was frowning, making him look stern and terrible, and every now and then, pain was tugging at his mouth. Apart from bruises and stiffness, she herself felt refreshed by her sleep. She was still filthy and encrusted with salt, and her ankle ached, but her worry for Carlo was greater than any physical pain of her own.

Sara came in with a steaming mug of coffee and a worried smile. She laid a plump brown hand on Carlo's forehead, and bit her lip.

'*Molto caldo,*' she whispered to Kate, brown eyes glistening. '*Febbre*—fever. Very bad.' Kate nodded her understanding, sipping gratefully at the hot coffee.

'You want—*dormire?*' Sara asked, pantomiming sleep.

'No, I'm fine,' she smiled. 'You get back to bed—and thanks for the coffee.'

The plump woman smiled, and went out, closing the door gently. Kate gazed down at Carlo, listening to the vicious anger of the wind. Her salty, muddy clothes were chafing her tender skin, and she glanced around the bedroom. Like her own, it had a bathroom and shower leading off it. She glanced at Carlo again, and decided to wash herself while he slept.

She found a fluffy dark-blue bathrobe hanging on the back of the door, and let herself silently into the black-tiled bathroom, with her coffee-mug in one hand. She drank the rest of her coffee under the shower, listening to the thunder that rumbled around the villa. If the storm continued for very much longer, she was under no illusions as to the danger Carlo would be in. The poison from his wound would begin to seep into his system, undermining even his iron constitution, and he would become very seriously ill. There had not been even a tube of penicillin cream in the first-aid box, and she was helpless to fight the infection. She stood naked in the shower, trying to relax.

The gentle heat soothed the ache out of bruises and the sting out of cuts and grazes. Her own pale body, which had just begun to become golden under the influence of the Mediterranean sun, was marked here and there with bruises and scratches, and her knees were like a naughty schoolgirl's. She rinsed the salt gratefully out of her hair letting the hot water run down her back. Her little bundle of filthy clothes looked out of place in the opulent bathroom, and she kicked the torn dress and underwear under the hot shower, hoping that the salt would rinse out of them. There was a full-length mirror set into the ebony tiles, and she checked herself for bruises in it. The expensive Catania haircut had survived the storm untouched, and she brushed the wet golden hair into place, remembering the way Carlo had appeared at the salon, and had taken her to see the sad graves.

She dried herself and her hair in one of the vast towels that hung in the bathroom, absently noting the simple, elegant toiletries that Carlo had left on the glass rail under the mirror—toothbrush, old-fashioned razor, a bottle of Chanel after-shave (given by whom? she wondered jealously), an old-fashioned wooden hairbrush. She found some talc, and dusted herself happily, revelling in the luxury of civilised comforts. She did not bother to look for perfume, but splashed a little of the Chanel on to her throat. Its spicy smell was delicious, and she remembered the night she had hung his overcoat up in her passageway, her heart thudding with virginal terror.

She opened the bathroom door silently, wrapped in the bathrobe that was four sizes too big for her, feeling greatly refreshed. Carlo's eyes flickered open, met hers with a tired glint. Kate padded quickly to his side and laid her hand on his forehead, wincing at the heat of his skin.

'How are you feeling?' she asked softly. He closed his eyes without answering, and a faint smile touched his marble lips. She sat down on the chair next to him, and wiped the beads of sweat gently off his face.

'You smell nice,' he whispered, his voice dry. His eyes opened again, and he turned his head to look at her, the formidable male light of his eyes undimmed by fever.

'Do you want some more aspirin?' she asked.

'In a while. Very hot . . .'

'Is your cut hurting you?'

'Numb . . .'

She shook some more paracetamol tablets into her hand, and offered them to him. He was too weak to take the glass, and she held it to his lips. Soon he was asleep. Within an hour he had begun to shiver uncontrollably, and the fierce white face on the pillow was wet. From time to time he moved restlessly, muttering in his fretful sleep. The fever had taken him under its wild spell, and Kate watched in horrified silence, fighting back her panic. Her own helplessnes filled her with impotent anger. She wiped the sweat off his forehead delicately.

'Don't die, darling,' she whispered, 'don't die—I love you so much . . .'

*

The Matron emerged from the isolation ward and came towards them, her hands folded in that way that matrons all over the world seem to learn, and spoke to them briefly in Italian. Lidia di Bari turned to Kate, her eyes concerned.

'They are worried about Carlo,' she said. 'They fear an infection of the blood—' She groped for the English word.

'Septicaemia?' ventured Kate. Lidia nodded, and Kate groaned in dismay. The tall, grey-bearded man who had been introduced as Carlo's lawyer shook his head sadly, and took Kate's arm in a gentle hand.

'Come, *signorina*—let us get something to eat.' The storm had broken early on the day before, and the party on Leparú had summoned the coastguard as soon as they could repair the radio mast. A motorboat had rushed Carlo, unconscious and raving, to the ultra-modern hospital at Catania. With characteristic Sicilian bluntness, the doctors had made it plain that Carlo was in danger of losing his life. After the senior consultant had also made it plain that without Kate's admittedly inadequate care, he would already be dead.

They walked down the hospital corridors to the canteen, a silent little group. Carlo's cousin Lidia had arrived from Palermo that morning, a handsome middle-aged woman whose Italian elegance had made Kate acutely aware of her own denim jeans and cheap yellow anorak. Dottore Bertorelli, the lawyer from Rome, had arrived soon afterwards. A subdued and tired-looking Vera completed the company. They sat down at one of the functional melamine tables in the primrose-yellow canteen, while Dottore Bertorelli went to get coffee and a brioche each for the three women.

Lidia di Bari lit a cigarette at Vera's gold lighter, blew out a plume of smoke, and smiled at Kate.

'So you are Caterina Melville,' she said, her grey eyes perusing Kate's face with interest. 'Ruggiero told us all so much about you. You are a painter, are you not?' She toyed absently with her gold bracelets as Kate explained her job briefly, then nodded.

'Your uncle was very proud of you, Caterina. You and Carlo were the only real friends he had, poor man.'

Kate looked at the beautiful, patrician face of the woman in front of her, and reflected that it was easy to understand how Roger had come to love her. The lawyer returned with a laden tray, and sat down with them. As they drank their coffees, he tugged nervously at his silvered beard.

'Without you, *signorina*, Carlo Castelli would now be dead.' He looked down at his brioche with unseeing eyes. 'We are all very grateful to you. Carlo is—a special person for many people.'

'He's very special to me,' she smiled sadly. The lawyer's clever eyes met hers, and then he and Lidia di Bari looked at one another.

'Signorina Melville,' he said frankly, 'I knew nothing of Carlo's involvement in this bizarre will of your uncle's until you told me the details this morning. It is a very strange business.'

'Roger Courtney was a strange man,' put in Vera. 'He adored practical jokes of this sort.'

'Undoubtedly,' mused Lidia, 'but this is one of the strangest things I have ever heard.' She glanced at Vera. 'Do you have any idea why Carlo should have agreed to make this extraordinary—*arrangement* concerning Leparú?'

'He wanted us to have the island,' said Vera over her coffee-cup, her dark eyes looking at the two Italians. 'That's what he said, wasn't it, Katherine?'

'Yes,' said Kate slowly. 'I never even contemplated the idea of marrying Carlo for the sake of a half-share in Leparú. It was just a holiday to me—a sort of crazy game.'

'If Carlo Castelli had wanted you to have Leparú,' said Dottore Bertorelli gravely, 'it would have been easier for him to have bought the island himself and given it to you, rather than go through the charade of a fake marriage.'

'Marriage is a serious business in Italy,' smiled Lidia. 'It's a Catholic country, and divorce is only obtainable with very great difficulty. It would take years, and cost thousands of pounds, in a case like this one.'

'Yes, but divorce is a lot easier and cheaper in Mexico,' said Vera archly. Then her face fell. 'Not that the idea seems such a good one right now,' she added.

'From what I know of Carlo,' said Lidia, 'I cannot imagine that he would easily agree to such a proposal. He did not take these things lightly.'

'I must agree,' added the lawyer, nodding at Kate. 'Carlo Castelli was very serious about such things as marriage—almost mystical, in fact. It is one of the traits of his character which he inherited from his grandmother— a mystical reverence for the rites of marriage and the sacredness of the marriage-bed. It is difficult to imagine that he was as unmoved by the idea as you report he was.' Kate stared at him in surprise, and he nodded. 'Oh, yes—I know that the idea repelled you, Signorina Melville; yet I cannot believe that it did not repel Carlo Castelli, too.' The lawyer rose, and bowed to the three women. 'I must go into Catania,' he said. 'Can I give anyone a lift?'

'Yes, please.' Vera rose, straightening her dress. 'I'm going to get back to Leparú—there's not much I can do here. I'll see you back on the island, Kate—there's a motorboat service from the jetty. So long—ring me if anything happens.' She and Bertorelli excused themselves, and walked off together.

Lidia watched them leave with calm grey eyes, then turned to Kate.

'You care very much about Carlo, don't you?' she asked gently. Kate nodded, trying not to let the tears spill out. The thought of Carlo in there, fighting for his life, was terrifying. The older woman patted her hand consolingly. 'Eat your brioche, my dear—your Carlo will be restored to you, I'm sure of that.'

Kate thought of the white, restless face on the stretcher the last time she had seen Carlo, and tried to smile. Lidia watched her for a few moments, then lit another cigarette, her beautiful gold bracelets jingling.

'I think I can explain a little about Carlo and this strange will to you, Caterina. I did not want to talk in front of Bertorelli or your cousin. Shall I try?'

'Please.' Kate sat back in the plastic chair, the sunlight washing over her face, and prepared to listen.

'Carlo Castelli is a lone wolf,' Lidia began, her eyes becoming introspective. 'Partly because he had a lonely childhood, but also because he is such an exceptional human being. Many women have thrown themselves at him, Caterina, but none have ever captured his heart.' She blew out smoke. 'I do not mean to deny that he has had affairs—a man with his looks and physique would naturally be able to take his pick—but he has never fallen under any woman's spell.'

Kate nibbled at her brioche, fascinated by what Lidia

was saying. 'Did—does he have many friends?' she asked.

Lidia shook her head. 'Not many. Acquaintances—yes, by the dozen. But true friends, very few. He and Roger met several times at my house in Palermo. Carlo may have told you,' she said, smiling sadly, 'that Ruggiero was an admirer of mine?'

'He said something about it,' Kate nodded.

'It was sad. Nevertheless, he and Carlo became good friends. My own interpretation was that Carlo saw in Ruggiero Courtney a father he had never known. And in Carlo, Ruggiero found a son. Did you know that your uncle helped Carlo to found his computer empire?' Kate shook her head, her eyes wide. 'Oh, yes. Ruggiero helped to finance the initial operations, some years ago. He had a little capital of his own, and such was his confidence in Carlo Castelli, that he invested almost all of it in Carlo's new design. That was how Carlo was able to begin manufacturing computers. And in return, Carlo made Ruggiero a rich man. Ruggiero sold his share in the company to Carlo some years ago, and bought Leparú. They were excellent friends, good companions.'

Kate stared out of the plate-glass window at the hospital's neat rose-garden, digesting this information.

'I knew nothing of all this,' she said at last. 'What do you think lies behind this strange will of Roger's, Lidia?'

'Who knows?' Lidia shrugged. 'As your cousin said, Ruggiero was a compulsive joker. That part of the story I cannot explain. But Carlo has obviously taken the will very seriously, Caterina. He is like that—a trust is sacred to him. He can be iron-willed about these things, even mystical, as Bertorelli said just now. To his family, his personal obligations, Carlo is utterly loyal. It may well be that he and Ruggiero had some private agreement regarding Leparú and the will—only Carlo can say. Yet he was devoted to Ruggiero, and his determination to fulfil the obligations of the will follows from that. He probably regards it as his duty to ensure that Leparú is divided between the two of you.'

'It's beginning to become clear to me,' sighed Kate, looking down at the bright yellow anorak she wore. 'But I wonder why—' She broke off. The Matron was hurrying towards them, her severe face concerned. She spoke to Lidia in low Italian, and the older woman stubbed out her cigarette at once, and stood up.

'Carlo is very ill,' she said, her face pale. 'But conscious. He wants to see you—at once.'

Kate gazed in wonder at the grim, white face on the hospital pillow.

'To marry me?' she repeated, stunned. 'But why?'

'Because of Leparú,' he answered, his voice little more than a whisper. Despite his physical weakness, his eyes were burning passionately. They held hers with an utter command, so that she could not look away. 'If I die, then Leparú will be lost,' he breathed. The fist that was clenched on the sheet was white-knuckled, and a pretty young nurse tried to soothe his forehead.

The drip that went into Carlo's strong brown arm frightened Kate. 'He is on intravenous antibiotics,' the doctor had warned her before she had gone into the isolation ward, 'he is very ill—do not tire him.' Carlo's opening words to her as she had gone in had struck to her heart like a dagger—*I want to marry you.*

'I don't care about Leparú,' she said urgently. 'I only care about you, Carlo—'

'Be still.' The complete authority in the whisper silenced Kate. 'I have sent for a priest already,' he said, the frighteningly luminous grey-green eyes holding hers. 'Will you do what I wish, Caterina?'

She looked up at the doctor's grave face, silently asking for help. The doctor nodded imperceptibly.

'Yes,' she said quietly, 'I will marry you, Carlo.' He closed his eyes, breathing so lightly that Kate's heart jumped with fear. She sat down to wait, thinking bitterly about the irony of the situation. The idea of marrying Carlo was so precious to her, so terribly important, that she had not even dared dream of it. And now that undreamed-of reality was here—but in what circumstances!

She stared around the little ward, her eyes blurring. She had come a long way since that morning in Mr Potter's dusty office, as she waited, almost bored, for the red-sealed will to be opened. And the magical story was ending in tragedy. She looked at Carlo's face, pale and terrible, and at the young nurse who was gazing down at him with a mixture of tenderness and compassion on her open face, wiping the sweat from his brow. Could he possibly survive? It seemed too cruel to be Carlo's widow, almost before she could be his bride. The door opened silently, and a young priest came in with the doctor, followed by Lidia. Catching sight of her, the priest came up to Kate. His face was almost boyish, and his dark, wise eyes met hers gently.

'Signorina Melville?'

'Yes—I'm Kate Melville.'

'Please tell me honestly—do you want to go through with this?'

'Yes,' she nodded sadly.

'Of your own free will? Not just to please the sick man?'

'I love him, Father,' she said simply.

His face cleared, but his eyes remained dark.

'Then come quickly.' She walked over to the side of the bed. Carlo's eyes opened, and lighted on the priest with a feverish brightness.

'Have you a ring?' the priest asked quietly. Kate shook her head. She knelt beside Carlo, and took his hand. 'We need a ring,' she said, her voice catching in her throat. He nodded, and his eyes held hers intently as he tugged weakly at the big gold signet ring that he wore on the little finger of his left hand. It was a heavy, antique thing, bearing a family crest on it. He put it into her hand, the fine gold glowing in the afternoon sun. She passed it to the priest, who laid it on the open page of his Bible with a nod of thanks. Kate held Carlo's hand tightly, trying to fathom his cloudy eyes.

'What are your first names?' the priest asked.

'Katherine Joan,' she answered, her throat aching with grief.

The priest smiled at her, his face compassionate. 'Is married to this man?' he asked gently. She shook her head. He repeated the question in Italian to Carlo, who shook his head, his eyes glowing in his white face.

'Then will you please repeat after me—"I, Katherine Joan."'

'I, Katherine Joan,' she whispered.

'Take thee, Carlo.'

'Take thee, Carlo . . .'

Outside the door of the ward, Kate gave way to her grief. Lidia put an arm around her and led her to a little seat in a sun-filled window.

'He may recover,' she told Kate softly. Kate nodded,

still crying, and gazed down at the heavy ring glittering on her wedding-finger. The doctor came out, and sat down next to Kate.

'Signora Castelli,' he said, and the name made Kate jump. He smiled sympathetically at her. 'Your husband is sleeping now. If septicaemia does not set in, then there is a chance he may yet recover. Do you understand that?'

'Yes—thank you, Doctor.'

'Perhaps your friend will take you to one of our restrooms—you can lie down for an hour or so. If you like I will send a nurse with something to help you sleep.'

'No, thank you,' she said unevenly. 'I'll be all right.'

Lidia walked her along the corridor to the little room at the end. With a motherly kiss on her forehead, she left Kate on the long couch, and went out.

Kate lay still, her tears spent. The gold ring was cold against her face. She shut her eyes, and tried to remember the colour of the sea on that first morning on Leparú, the sound of Carlo's mocking voice against the waves as he praised her body—'like a courtesan in a Bronzino painting.' Now he was facing death, waging a long, grim struggle, and she was unable to be with him. With the supreme irony of one of Roger Courtney's wild pranks, she was married to a dying man—a man to whom she was of no more significance than an act of duty to a dead friend.

Yet against the stark background of his mortal peril, Carlo Castelli had become more sharply-defined in her mind. That afternoon at Casa Botticelli had showed her that she loved him; but it was the prospect of his dying that had revealed to her—cruelly—how deep her love was. If the gut-wrenching fear she felt now was a true indication, then she loved Carlo as she would never love another human being. Sleep stole up on her unawares . . .

'Signora Castelli?'

She awoke to find Dottore Bertorelli standing next to her. She sat up, asking, 'How is he?'

'Much the same, *signora*. I saw him a few minutes ago, and he was in a coma. By the way, may I congratulate you on your marriage?'

She took his hand, suddenly aware of her pale plastic anorak, her tousled hair.

'Thank you,' she said drily. 'This is scarcely the happiest day of my life, *dottore*.'

'Of course, of course,' he said. 'But we must all have hope, no?' He sat down on the chair next to the bed, opening his briefcase. 'You are now Carlo's next of kin,' he said, looking at her carefully. 'You do understand that?'

'I hadn't thought of it,' she admitted.

'It means—please excuse me for mentioning this, *signora*—that in the event of Carlo's death, you will inherit his whole estate. And in the meantime, there are many decisions to be made. One of them concerns the island.'

'Leparú? What about it?'

'I saw Carlo a short while after the—er—marriage, and he instructed me to make arrangements to dispose of Leparú immediately. The island will be sold at auction next week, and the proceeds are to be divided between your cousin Vera de Cruz and yourself.'

'I see.'

'I hope you have no objections?'

'Not if it's Carlo's wish,' she said simply.

'Excellent,' said the lawyer. 'Even after the sale of the island, several weeks will elapse before the transfer to its new owner will be complete. If you wish, therefore, you will be able to continue living at the villa there. Unless you would prefer me to find you a hotel here in Catania?'

'No, that won't be necessary,' she said briefly.

'Very well, *signora*.' The lawyer's thin, distinguished face took on an almost embarrassed look, and he tugged awkwardly at his white beard.

'Was there something else, *dottore*?' Kate asked gently.

The lawyer nodded, looking unhappy.

'There *was* something else which your husband requested, *signora*. I hope it will not offend you—he has requested that you stay away from the hospital completely from now on.'

'I see,' said Kate bitterly.

The lawyer met her eyes sympathetically. 'Your husband will send for you when he wishes to see you,' he said.

'He'll send for me, will he?' Kate asked with sour irony. She twisted the heavy gold signet ring on her finger. 'Am I not even to be allowed to visit my husband's bedside, then?'

'In Italy,' said Dottore Bertorelli placatingly, 'wives are very obedient to their husbands' wishes.'

'Are they indeed?' snapped Kate. She tugged her anorak straight and walked over to the door, her heart aching with the double hurt of Carlo's illness and this last snub. 'Will you tell my husband, then, that when he condescends to see me, I'll be on Leparú?' The lawyer bowed, plainly discomfited, and Kate walked blindly down the corridor.

CHAPTER TEN

The Mediterranean was an aquamarine blue as blue as a sea of cornflowers. The taxi that was carrying Kate to the hotel was driving along the sea-front from the dock, and she stared out of the window with absent eyes. She twisted the heavy masculine ring on her finger, a gesture she had performed countless numbers of times since her marriage ten days ago. Oddly, the ring had fitted her perfectly—it even had a strange beauty against her slender hand—and it was not for any physical discomfort that she twisted it nervously, to and fro, to and fro.

She had been living on Leparú since then, alone with Rosario and Sara, who had treated her with compassionate awe since she had returned. She had spent the time trying not to think, alone with the mild blue sea that had so nearly claimed Carlo's life. Nearly—but not quite. The first news that he was recovering had come a week earlier, bringing Kate an unspeakable relief. And to-day, the imperious summons had come from the hospital—*your husband wishes to see you.* Like a dutiful Italian wife, she had come, leaving the watercolour she had started fluttering on its easel on the white beach.

She twisted the ring nervously. She had examined the finely-engraved coat of arms, with its proud stag's head, so often that she felt she could have drawn it with her eyes shut. And now it was going back to its true owner.

Leparú had been sold. Dottore Bertorelli had come to tell them that an oil millionaire from Texas had purchased it for just under a quarter of a billion lire—two hundred and forty thousand pounds. He had presented Vera and Kate with a cheque apiece for half that sum. Vera, well satisfied, had left for London at once, without even waiting to hear whether Carlo was recovering or not. To Kate's faint surprise, there had been no malice in Vera's farewells at the airport.

'I thought I had a chance with Carlo Castelli,' she had said. 'It doesn't matter now—I've got my share of Leparú, and anyway, you can't trust men, can you?'

'I suppose not,' Kate had answered absently.

'You've done the right thing, Mrs Castelli,' Vera had smiled. 'You'll be quids in, whether he pops it or not. I'm happy with my hundred and twenty thou—it'll keep me in furs for a while!'

Kate had seen her off without regrets, and had returned quietly to Leparú, and the watercolours that she had at last unpacked from her case. And the first thing that had come from her brush had been a splendid golden face with piercing grey-green eyes and a laughing mouth. Carlo had been right after all—love *had* transformed her vision of the world, and for the first time it seemed to Kate that her own paintings were brimming with colour and life. And Beth Hussey had been right too—the light on Leparú *was* different. It flooded the painting she had made of Carlo, making it so very obviously a labour of love. Unable to destroy it as she had wished to, she had thrust the painting into a portfolio, trying to bury it with her aching love.

Well, the turbulent holiday was at an end. She was under no illusions as to what the arrogant summons from Carlo portended—he would explain to her, as gently as he could, that everything was now over, that the divorce in Reno, or Brazil, or wherever the fashionable place for quickie divorces was nowadays, must soon follow.

'*Ospedale, signora.*' The taxi pulled up at the front of the sprawling modern hospital, and she paid her fare absent-mindedly. The roses outside the canteen nodded their wise, beautiful heads at her as she walked up the steps, telling herself not to cry, not to grow angry, and not to show Carlo Castelli by so much as a wince how desperately badly he was going to hurt her. She had dressed as simply as she knew how for this interview, with a white cotton skirt that covered the scratches still healing on her knees.

Her heart was thudding as she pushed open the door of Carlo's private room. He was sitting in a deck-chair by the open window, the sun glowing in the dark skin of his stomach, visible through the open top of his pyjamas. He heard the tiny sound of the door opening, and turned to face her.

The magnificent eyes jolted her square in the heart, as they had always done, always would do. He stood a little stiffly as she came towards him, her mouth dry. He looked so well! The terrible pallor was gone, and so was the tenseness in his face. The lazy, mocking smile that met her was burning with energy.

'You wish to see me,' Kate said, as coldly as she could.

'You are my wife, *cara*,' he purred, his eyes flicking over her body with insolent amusement.

'Indeed,' she retorted, 'and here I am, an obedient slave to your will. What was it you wanted?'

'Are you not going to kiss your husband?'

'Carlo,' she gritted, 'say what you have to say—but don't play with me.'

'Play with you?' he asked in mock-surprise, coming over to her. 'Is a kiss on greeting not one of the accepted marital privileges?' He raised her chin with his hand, and kissed her tightly-compressed lips lightly. 'Ah, little ice-maiden! Such reserve no longer becomes you, *cara*. You are a married woman, and you must learn to melt a little in the flame of passion!'

'So—you are going to begin exercising your marital privileges?' she asked with soft anger, rubbing her mouth as if to rub his kiss off her lips.

'Sooner than you expect,' he said, with a heart-stopping smile. 'I am being discharged to-day.'

'Are you better already?' she asked anxiously, her eyes dropping to the pad of white gauze across his ribs.

Carlo looked carefully into her face.

'I can go home,' he told her, 'as long as you agree to change the dressings for me. Can you do that?'

'If you wish me to,' she said shortly, trying to conceal the trembling in her legs that his proximity had brought on. It was extraordinary that he could not see her love, her unashamed desire for him, burning in her clear eyes.

'*Brava,*' he said with an ironic smile. 'I hope the act will not turn your delicate stomach.'

'How can you be so mocking,' she retorted angrily, 'when *I* bandaged it the first time, in the midst of the storm?'

'True,' he smiled. 'Yet then your face did not wear the anger and disgust it wears now.'

Kate tore her gaze away from the erotic message in his eyes, and twisted the heavy ring on her finger bitterly.

'You were cruel to send me away from the hospital, Carlo. I was worried sick for you—I had no idea whether you would live or die, whether you were getting better, or sinking—' She broke off, her voice trembling.

'It made a difference to you, then?'

'Don't be a fool,' she said shakily. 'You didn't have to exile me from your side, Carlo. I have no illusions about our marriage.'

'Indeed?' he asked softly.

'I'm no fool,' she said drily. 'You didn't need to snub me like that to give me the message.'

'What message, my dear Caterina?' he asked quietly.

'The message that our marriage was merely an obligation to Roger Courtney, nothing more.' Abruptly she twisted the gold ring off her finger, an act that tore at her very heart, and held it out to him. 'Here's your ring back,' she said.

'Put it back!' His eyes were blazing with a terrifying anger. She gaped at him for a moment. *'Do as I say!'* he snarled, moving towards her with an almost threatening air. Kate slid the ring back on to her finger, her heart thumping. 'If you ever take it off again,' he said, his face cold and furious, 'I'll put you over my knee and thrash you.' He drew a deep breath. 'That was the only thing that came to me from my father, Caterina mine. It is no bauble, but your true wedding ring.'

'But, Carlo,' she stammered, her mouth dry, 'I understand what you want—'

'You understand nothing,' he said in a grating voice. 'You have much to learn, *cara*—about yourself, and about your husband.'

'You take this mockery beyond a joke,' she snapped, her voice strained and bitter. 'Do you like to torment me, like a cruel boy with a bird?'

'Madre di Dio,' he raged, 'are you deaf, dumb, and blind? God grant that I have not married a complete fool! How must I tell you? With drawings? With sign language? We are *married*, Caterina!'

'What can you mean?' she asked shakily.

'I find this all slightly tedious,' he said, pulling his shirt off. 'We are going back to Leparú—I shall have to show you what I mean there.'

'But Leparú has been sold,' she said faintly.

'To an American millionaire? I am that man,' he said shortly. 'Go and tell the Matron that I'm discharging myself,' he commanded, 'and then telephone the Chryscraft agents at the docks, and tell them we'll be picking up the new boat in an hour.' He turned to her, his splendid torso naked except for the square of gauze on his flank. 'Don't just stand there gaping,' he snapped. 'Run!'

She ran.

The late afternoon sun was warm and golden on their naked skin. The long-drawn sigh of the sea drifted up the beach, as they lay in the hot sand. Kate watched Carlo's face with something akin to awe, her heart thudding in her throat.

'Then—you don't want to divorce me?' she asked timidly.

'Divorce?' he repeated, his mouth mocking. 'Has no one told you that you've married a Catholic? I may not be a very good one, but I certainly don't permit the word "divorce" in my family.' He rolled over on to his good side and looked into her eyes with the bone-melting intensity she had first learned to love.

Losing herself in the grey-green depths, Kate whispered, 'I think I'm dreaming . . .'

'No dream, *cara*.' His finger traced a line from the corner of her eye to the corner of her quivering mouth. 'I love you, Caterina Castelli.'

'Carlo—darling—I love you so very much.'

His lips were as warm and as deep as a sun-warmed sea. Suddenly her mind was tired of asking why, of trying to explain the miracle that had happened to her. She surrendered to the complete authority of his kiss, her arm sliding around his strong neck, her lips meeting his, timidly, adoringly, passionately.

'I've loved you since you came into my little flat that night, and told me about the volcano,' she whispered, her voice soft as the sigh of the sea.

'I loved you first when you grew so angry at the St James',' he smiled.

'Then my love is a day older than yours!'

'But not a fathom deeper.' He kissed her again, but not gently this time, so that she was suddenly panting, her face flushed and amorous.

'There,' he said, his smile wicked, 'that's another piece of ice melted.'

'I don't know if I'm ever going to forgive you for flirting with Vera like that,' Kate said against his chest.

'I wouldn't call it flirting,' he grinned. 'It was more a way of getting you jealous—just to find out what you really felt about me.'

'Oh, really? And what if Vera had fallen in love with you?'

'Vera's got a heart of microchips and circuits, like one of my computers,' he replied drily. 'She wasn't in any danger.'

Kate sighed.

'I don't deserve this, my darling—not you, not the island, not any of it.'

'Once I promised to tell you one day what I thought of your story,' he said gently. 'Remember? It was quite a story, Caterina. I was ready to love you even before I saw your dear face, and touched your dear lips. Remember, I'd followed the story for five years, through the letters you sent Roger. When I came to find you, I was expecting the pale little girl of the photographs you sent your uncle— thin and worried-looking. I wasn't prepared for your beauty, *cara*, for your quickness and grace. And especially not,' he added softly, brushing her eyelids with his lips, 'for the way you affected me physically.'

'Really?' she asked with innocent surprise and pleasure.

'Really,' he smiled, his eyes an intimate caress on her face. 'It hasn't been easy keeping myself in check all these weeks. It's taken a lot of cold showers and a lot of deep breathing.' The scarlet tide that swept into her cheeks made him roar with laughter.

'I wonder if I'll ever learn not to do that?' she murmured, burying her face against his chest.

'I hope I shall be making you blush when we're both in our eighties,' he smiled lovingly. Kate looked up at him again with worshipping eyes.

'Why did you come to find me, Carlo?'

'It was Roger's wish,' he said gently. 'I owe Roger a great deal, Caterina. He was like a father to me in many ways, mischievous as he was. In his last months he became obsessed with the hope of leaving you Leparú— and of your marrying me.'

'No!' she gasped.

'Yes,' he smiled. 'It was his last dream, *cara*. That is why he made that strange will.'

'But Vera—?'

'Roger was no fool,' he answered, gazing out across the setting sun. 'At first he toyed with the idea of leaving you the island on condition that you married me. But then he realised that you would be too wilful, too strong to succumb to such a bribe. So he devised the idea of splitting the island between you and Vera, his only other relative. His idea was that once you and I met, we would immediately fall in love with one another. For some reason, he was convinced that we were perfectly suited to one another.'

'What an extraordinary man!' she breathed, following his gaze to the orange splendour of the setting sun.

'Yes, he was extroardinary. It was one of the brain-waves of his last months, *cara*, to bring us together—the two humans in all the world who had returned his love. And like all Roger's jokes, this one had a deeper meaning, a special significance.'

'Did you know this all along?'

'Not in full,' he said, the sun gilding his face as he turned to give her his wonderful smile. 'When old Mr Potter told me the terms of Roger's will, I was as taken aback as you were. But from the cryptic letter he left me, and from years of being the amused victim of his jokes, I was able to work out what he had in mind.'

'So Vera was simply a decoy—to divert attention from the real point of the joke?'

'Which was to bring us together in a ridiculous inhibition-destroying situation. Yes. And Leparú itself was just a decoy, too—simply a stage on which to place two characters.'

'A lovely stage, darling, and a lovely plot.'

'The plot was our own,' he smiled, touching her lips with his finger. 'Roger was simply the stage-manager—a shadowy author in the wings . All he wanted to do was to throw us together, involve us both in some crazy situation. In the hope that we would fall in love.'

'As we have done.'

'Yes,' he said quietly, 'as we have done.'

Kate's eyes were blurred, and the sunset blazed into scarlet and crimson fires through the prism of her tears.

'Don't cry,' Carlo murmured against her cheek. 'At the end of a good romantic comedy, you should smile.'

'I'm trying,' she said shakily. 'I love you, Carlo.'

He laid her gently, down, and kissed the soft flower of her mouth. She gazed up at him, lovesick for his touch.

'Then—you asked Dottore Bertorelli to buy the island?'

'Yes,' he nodded. 'I want it to be here for us always, Caterina—a place for our children, a place to come to when Rome gets too much for us. I had to work out a way of ensuring that Vera got her inheritance—and she seems to be happy.'

'She is,' confirmed Kate. 'And the island is really ours?'

'Leparú is your wedding present,' he said quietly.

'But then I still have a hundred thousand pounds that belongs to you!'

'I know it's a little late,' he grinned, 'but you're going to need some kind of a trousseau. You can't go around in a yellow anorak all your life.'

'That was my wedding dress!'

'And we haven't even got a picture,' he mocked. 'When we go back to Rome, you will want furs and diamonds, like all Roman women.'

'And you make me buy them myself,' Kate mocked in return, 'like a true Roman husband!' She smothered his laugh with a kiss. 'Will I like Rome, Carlo?'

'You will love it. I have my flat there—it's a small, austere place. No doubt you will want a small palace somewhere.'

'You think I'll be extravagant?'

'I shall insist on it,' he smiled.

She traced the long red scar on his flank with a fingertip, and the ripple of gooseflesh that spread over the golden skin made her own stomach muscles contract with sympathetic desire. 'Why did you send me away from the hospital?' she whispered. 'It nearly broke my heart.'

'I could not bear the thought of your having to watch me die,' he said gently.

'Idiot!' she said, her eyes reflecting the crimson rose of the sunset. 'Did you think it would make my worry any easier?'

'Perhaps I was wrong,' Carlo confessed.

'A miracle,' she smiled. 'Carlo Castelli admits that he's wrong!'

'To change the subject,' he said, his voice a deep purr, 'this bikini of yours has fascinated me ever since I first saw you in it.' He tugged at the thin golden strap that secured the top, and Kate gasped.

'Rosario and Sara—'

'Have gone to bed, as all married couples should do on a day like this.'

'But Carlo—'

'Besides,' he growled, 'it's dark and warm . . .'

She gasped again, in a different way, as his lips touched her flesh, finding the places where pleasure lay waiting, with delicious sensuality.

'Carlo,' she moaned, 'this isn't decent!'

He looked up, estimating the distance to the villa.

'I might just make it,' he growled. 'And the bed *is* more traditional. Shall we run?'

Harlequin® Plus

THE STORY OF DON JUAN

When the Spanish monk Tirso de Molina put pen to paper in 1630, he gave life to Europe's most notorious playboy, Don Juan, with whom Carlo is compared. With eyes as black as his skintight garb, Don Juan broke the heart of one woman after another. This irresistible scoundrel, who never fell in love, was the first of many incarnations of a colorful character known throughout Europe since the Middle Ages.

In Molina's play, the handsome nobleman tries to seduce the daughter of a knight. When the knight challenges him to a duel, Don Juan wins and later mockingly invites the statue on his victim's tomb to dinner. The statue accepts, then returns the favor—but instead of a meal Don Juan is whisked to Hell.

This literary legend hopscotched his way through Europe, appearing in Italian theater and in a French comedy by Molière as a more thoughtful, less passionate *homme fatal*. But even this version of the Latin lover was too irreverent for the Parisian clergy, and they closed the play after a few performances. Don Juan reappeared in Mozart's *Don Giovanni,* amorously bounding into the hearts of opera lovers.

In the nineteenth century, the romantic poet Lord Byron, a bit of a rascal himself, wrote *Don Juan,* one of the longest satirical poems in the English language. His character is a naive mischievous fellow whose adventurous spirit leads him into a shipwreck with pirates, a harem and the arms of Catherine the Great of Russia. Eventually Don Juan goes on a diplomatic mission to England, and Byron uses the scenario to poke fun at British society.

Don Juan comes full circle in a nineteenth-century play by José Zorrilla. In it a beautiful woman changes the selfish romancer into a man capable of love.

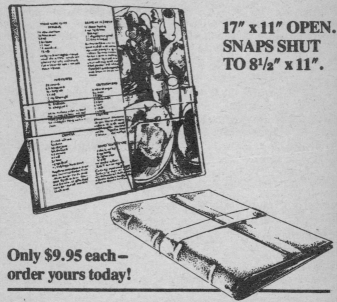